MY BLOOD RUNS BLUE

BOOK 1 IN THE MY BLOOD RUNS BLUE SERIES

STACY EATON

NITEWOLF NOVELS

ACKNOWLEDGMENTS

The day I started this book I looked at my husband and told him, "I'm writing a book." His eyebrows rose and he said, "Okay." He never said another word about that, and when I handed him a few chapters to read a couple of days later, he didn't seem exactly excited, but being the incredible husband that he is, he started reading, and giving me his input.

So my first thank you goes to him. Thank you for standing beside me, or more like sitting beside me in the office, while I typed on and on. Thank you for supporting me as I began this venture and for believing in me, always.

Thanks go out to my cousin Anne who was actually the third one to read my book and add her helpful comments and suggestions.

Many thanks are being sent to my friend Gregory Shannon who read every word I wrote and put me on the track to making this book make sense. Your humor about "then" and "than" kept me on my toes, along with the time you took to do research about some of the things I had written. I so appreciate the time you spent helping me out! I look forward to your input on my second book.

Thank you also to my Gemini Justice Sisters...while you two

didn't make it into book one, I have awesome plans for you in book two!

There are so many others to thank: my friends, my co-workers, family members, my "Seasters," and even my dogs. You have inspired me and helped me to create a story that I hope all of you will enjoy! Thank you for standing by me!

My last thanks go to my children. I know my son wasn't crazy about me writing about vampires if there were no werewolves in the story, but I think he will still be proud of me. And to my treasured princess, while you can't read this book now, when you grow up, may you read this and enjoy the words I have written. I love you both.

CHAPTER ONE

KRISTIN

Sometimes it felt as though I was driving in circles around my township, especially at night. I drove aimlessly, peering out the windows of my patrol car at the private homes, lonely winding roads, and deeply-shadowed woods. Many officers thought the night shift sucked because of all the quiet time. Sometimes I agreed. When there was so much downtime in the deep of night, the nightmares buried deeply inside slithered and threatened to strangle me. There was so much time behind the wheel of my patrol car; watching—waiting—and allowing my mind to drift.

Ten years ago, I started the job here. I was twenty-four then. Some nights I felt as though I could close my eyes and still manage to drive the twists and turns of the lightless country roads. I'd driven thousands of miles during daylight and in the murkiness of night on these streets. Many times, I had a mission in mind. Others, I wandered pointlessly and tried to find something to keep me occupied. I often wondered if I was trying to find myself—or better yet—lose myself. Tonight, while dwelling on these exact thoughts, a favorite song of mine came on the radio.

The haunting melody floated through the car's speakers and occupied my mind with thoughts of someone forgetting me—missing me.

Missing me? Well, maybe not exactly. Occasionally, I felt like someone *was actually* missing me. As if there was somebody out there who called to my very soul and would provide it with a real purpose, one I had yet to discover.

Maybe it was because I missed Trevor, although this feeling had been with me for longer than the past two years since he died.

Or it could've been because my mother was killed when I was an infant and I never knew my father. I continuously felt as if I should be searching for something more or someone to complete me.

Whatever...

I was a strong woman! I needed no one to complete me! I had friends and co-workers, and a job that kept my mind busy and my body active—who needed more than that, right?

Who was I kidding? I snorted in the empty car. I was lonely as hell, and as hard as I tried not to be, I was sad to be by myself in this life. I stared through the dark windshield; what waited for me out there? I believed that everything had a purpose in life, and I was seriously ready to unearth mine.

I have always been a person who felt the need to control their destiny. A person who made a decision based on where it would take them in life. My biggest strength: I was a control freak. I took command of the things around me, and when done correctly, it propelled me forward in life and helped those around me, too.

My biggest downfall: I was a control freak. I would be the first one to admit that this same strength got me in trouble all the time. Sometimes it was hard to stop needing to dominate everything and move along with the flow. This particular flaw was what held me back at the time, kept me from finding someone else to have in my life and to love. I was so afraid to love someone else and run the chance of losing that restraint—and the other person—again.

The loud sounds of a recent number one song filled the car and I reached for my phone as it lit up. It was probably my partner, Mick. He was one of the few people I knew who'd be awake at this time of night. I glanced at the screen, yep. I brought the phone to my ear, automatically answering it when I did so. "What's up?" I asked, trying to keep my voice upbeat when I felt anything but.

"Hey, you eat yet?" The strong yet soft voice of my partner vibrated my ear drum.

"Nope, was thinking about heading nineteen to do just that," I lied. I wasn't hungry but being in the light of the station might keep me from wallowing in the dank pit of self-pity I was sinking into.

"K. I'll meet you nineteen—whoever gets there first, starts the coffee. Looks like we're gonna need it tonight. Quiet out here."

I cringed. "Jesus, Mick—thanks. There goes our night now." Everyone on the job knew that you never said the "Q" word. It was the biggest jinx in the world. "Fine, I'll see you at the station in a few." I dropped my phone in the cup holder of my console beside me and turned left onto a road that would eventually take me back to the station.

I might have complained about the dark, but driving in it was a heady feeling, at least to me. Most nights, I thrived working the night shift. The shift would generally start with the sun low in the west, and I'd work through the dead of night to keep the residents protected. Then I'd go home in the morning feeling a sense of satisfaction that I'd done my job. The residents didn't need to know what traveled the roadways at night, or the people whom I dealt with in the shadows. They just needed to know they were safe to go about their lives.

I pulled up to the station and was backing into my regular spot when Mick zipped into the driveway. Driveway, yes, to our station—to our home, and it was home. It was a regular little ranch house that had been converted to a small police station by a local developer looking for a tax write-off. It was small, but for the most part, it worked for us. We were a tiny department, only eight officers, plus Chief Henderson and our Admin Assistant, Kat Peterson.

It got pretty crowded in the station when we were all there, but that only happened once in a great while and usually when something big happened or a meeting was called. Otherwise, it worked with the three or four of us who traveled around within the small rooms. We were used to the dancing that was required to get around each other, especially while wearing our duty gear.

I climbed out of the Expedition, my current patrol vehicle, and took a moment to appreciate my partner as he exited his Charger. When some people saw him, they stopped dead in their tracks and stared wide-eyed. He wasn't tall. He was my height—about five foot five—but he was wide, at least twice my width and his face had a dark, aggressive look that made people think twice before they did something stupid. After lifting weights for twenty years, he was able to move within his strong body fast and gracefully, despite his bulk. He was attractive in an obscure and stormy kind of way, and extremely quiet, especially if he didn't know you.

Mick and I had been partners for years, and as I observed him, I was honored to know he was my partner, proud to call him my friend and my brother in blue. There was no sexual interest between us; we were friends, partners, co-workers.

"You do know if we get any calls tonight, they are going to you first since you just jinxed the shit out of us." I grinned as I spoke. He guffawed, because he knew that if a call were dispatched, then I would be by his side, no matter what I said.

"Yep, I got them *all* tonight." His laughter followed us to the door where I pulled my keys off my belt.

I put a small piece of plastic up to a numeric pad next to the heavy industrial door; a small thump let me know the magnetic lock had been released, and Mick pulled the door open, holding it for me to precede him through. The entrance led into the back of our station, which constituted as our locker room, equipment storage room, and evidence processing area. Yep, all that rolled into a small area of about twenty feet in length and twelve feet wide. We used our space exceptionally well.

Mick followed me through the locker room and into the kitchen area, where we had traded the old stove for two large four-drawer filing cabinets. The rest of the kitchen included two counters, a standard sink, cabinets, a microwave, a regular-sized refrigerator, and of course, our beloved coffee maker.

I walked over to our life-giving machine and flipped open the top, pulling out the old grounds, while Mick reached into a cabinet and took down the container of coffee. We worked as a team; we always did. No words were spoken. We didn't need them; we had this down to a science. Once the coffee was brewing, we went about washing our hands and pulling our food out of the fridge.

"Hey, you mind if I put on the game?" Mick asked. Why he had bothered, I had no clue. Whether we were watching it or not, there was always some sporting event playing on the big flat-screen TV above our heads in the patrol area.

Our patrol area was actually the living room of the old house. A large counter separated the small waiting area in the front of the L-shaped desk that ran across the room and along the wall toward the kitchen. The desk contained several computers and a Mobile Data Terminal, known to us as an MDT, that was hooked up to our County Dispatch system. The TV hung on the wall in the waiting area and could be seen from any angle in the patrol or kitchen area.

I didn't bother to answer because I knew he already had the controller in hand and was hitting the power button as he spoke.

We sat at the small round table on the side of the kitchen and pulled out our sandwiches. His were lovingly made by his wife and consisted of two monstrous meatloaf sandwiches on whole wheat bread. Mine came from the local deli—a quick, easy meal since I never cooked anymore, and had no one to cook for anyway. I sighed without meaning to.

"What's up?" Mick glanced at me as he chomped another mouthful. He might have had one eye on the game, but he was usually aware of my moods.

"Nothing," I replied. "Just another night, ya know?" I wasn't going to explain that once again, as I thought of his loving wife, thoughts of my own depressing life haunted me. The loss that I dealt with, the loneliness that stayed with me on a constant basis. The nightmares I had of the night they came to tell me. The other odd dreams that I'd had for years that somehow seemed so damn real—but were just out of my grasp of understanding; dreams that grew more confusing and had now become somewhat of a daily occurrence.

His mammoth shoulders rose in a shrug. He knew I wasn't telling the truth, but he also understood that if I wanted to discuss it, I would.

I examined the ham sandwich I had unrolled from the deli paper. I really wasn't hungry, but I knew I should eat. My teeth were just sinking into the Kaiser roll when my lapel mic came to life with three tones and the female voice of "Thirty-One units."

Son-of-a-bitch!

CHAPTER TWO

JULIAN

"Jules... Thanks for coming on such short notice," Alexander stated as I entered the room.

Yeah, like I had a fucking choice, I thought. "Yes, of course, sir. I came as soon as I got your text message." He knew I was lying. I had actually put off showing up for almost two hours. I always dreaded coming to see my boss. Once my best friend, he was now just the person I took my orders from. There was a lot of tension coiled around us, and even after forty years, you could still feel it in the air when we were in the same room. He would never forgive me—I would never forgive myself.

Alexander locked his arrogant eyes on me. I saw the skin around them tighten while his jaw clenched. I leaned back in the black leather chair across from his desk with a calm expression and crossed my right leg over my left, resting my ankle on my knee. I waited, looking him straight in the eye, and tried to appear relaxed, even though I was wound tight and ready to explode. But he knew that, no matter how calm I seemed.

Dark green eyes, the deep rich color of emeralds, regarded me from a strong, solid face. Long brown wavy hair fell to his shoulders and surrounded his angular features. He was wearing one of his normal suits, and as usual, no tie. Most people would have taken the jacket off to sit at their own desk, but not Alexander. I couldn't remember the last time I had seen him without his suit coat on. But then again, I avoided him at all costs these days.

The office where we met was filled with expensive decor, including a dark cherry desk with matching chairs. The cherry frames on the wall held expensive original works of art. The entire room was done in deep rich colors showing taste and elegance all at once. No windows—none at all. But our type didn't like windows; we avoided the sunlight whenever possible.

Finally, Alexander rolled his shoulders and continued. "Jules, I know you've been working on this case for a while, trying to locate Damon." He paused and tapped a pen on his desk twice before leaning back in his chair. "Well, it appears he has finally surfaced again." He was regarding me closely to see how the words would affect me.

As much as I hated to react around Alex, my eyes widened for a mere fraction of a second, and I stiffened. Pure hate coursed through my veins, my eyeteeth slowly lengthening at the mention of his name. Damon. We had been searching for him for thirty-seven years, waiting to find him and drive a stake through his evil heart.

I controlled my emotions the best I could and took a slow deep breath, making sure my teeth had retracted before answering. "Where?" was all I could get out through my tightly pressed lips.

Alexander knew that I was trying to retain control. If anyone knew the hatred I felt for Damon, it was him. It was something we shared—the only thing we shared these days. He didn't have to hear inside my mind or see my expression; he could feel my emotions. It was one of his many gifts. He knew I wanted nothing more than to find Damon and end his existence…forever.

"It appears that he might be in eastern Pennsylvania. Our sources say there have been some attacks on our kind in an area west of Philadelphia. It's his normal pattern of killing." He waited to take in my reaction. When he got none, he continued. "We aren't certain that they are all from our breed, but the ones we have been able to confirm, look to be ours."

So close—he was so damn close right now. Just across the state line of New York lay Pennsylvania. I knew his behavior, knew it all too well; I had fallen victim to it. No, not myself, but people I'd loved. People I would never see again: my wife and love of my life, Calista, and our beautiful five-year-old daughter, Anastasia.

"Julian, if you want someone else to go after him, I can send Gabe —" he started to say.

"No, Alexander, I can do this alone. I want him. I need to finish this myself," I was quick to reply.

"You're taking this personally, Jules." He put his hand up to stop me when I would have interrupted. "You know it is better to not have a personal attachment to your assignment. I have allowed you to stay on this case because I know how good you are and how focused you can be. I also figure that maybe your attachment to him might help you locate him, to allow us to finally grieve and move on." He looked down at his desk, knowing he had made a mistake in his words as he fingered the expensive pen in his hand.

I caught the "us" in there. *Yeah, you loved her, too. But she chose me.*

I couldn't repress the sigh as I looked down at the beautifully hand-sewn Oriental rug at my feet, not really seeing it, but noticing its bright reds and blues, the same colors that were swirling around in my mind. Red for hatred and blue for the loss I had suffered. I was taking it personally, I knew that, but I would not allow any other warrior to find Damon and take him to the other world. This would be my vengeance, and mine alone.

I looked back at him with that heated emotion stark in my expression as he continued.

He tried to redeem his words, and I almost laughed. "We cannot allow Damon to keep up with this behavior. Killing our females and children is not what we are about. If he continues, our race will end."

"Master, I know it is not. I will be fine; I can distance myself from the attachment. You, of all people, know that," I said calmly.

"Fine, so be it, but Gabriel is going with you this time," he said, with a flick of his hand.

"You don't need to send a babysitter with me, Alexander," I retorted, as anger bubbled under my skin.

He regarded me with a quick tight-lipped expression that told me he was about to lose his cool. "It is not to watch over you, Julian. It is to assist you. Stop being so damn stubborn. I want this stopped, now. Too many females and children have died over the last thirty-seven years, and while it appears that he was dormant for a while, he is starting to go after them again now. Stop him. Stop him before he destroys us."

"I'm sorry." I hung my head as was expected of me. "Master Alexander—fine. I will accept the help." I knew when to argue and when not to and arguing with him right now would only get me thrown off the case completely. At least it was Gabriel who would be with me, and not Alex.

"Where are we going, and when?" I asked quietly.

"Fawn Hollow." He stated softly and watched me intently. "The VMF still owns the property there. You do remember *that* house, don't you?" His eyes sparked with anger. Of course, I remembered the house. It was where my life had changed, and it was also the place where our friendship had ended.

His chest rose and fell before he continued. "It will make it easy for you to keep to yourselves without anyone noticing your doings. The police force in that area is small, so they shouldn't be a problem. The house is being prepared for you as we speak. You can take your own car and head down at sunset."

Alex stood and I knew I was dismissed. I had been good about controlling my emotions while I was here with him. I could allow my walls to drop now.

I unfolded my leg and braced my hands on the arms of the leather chair to push myself up. We stood regarding each other over the top of the desk. If he had not been my boss, if it had not been for our mutual love of Calista, we might have still been friends. Many years ago, it would've been him to assist me on this task.

"Go now, Jules. Find him. End this," he said quietly.

"Yes, Master Alexander, I will." I turned and headed for the door.

Alexander called out, "Be swift and safe…and finish this, Jules. You owe it to her. You owe it to all of us."

I hung my head on a sigh. "I will, Alex. Thank you." I nodded once and left the room without looking back.

CHAPTER THREE

KRISTIN

*S*hit...shit...shit! Really! Tones and both units... "Thirty-One-Paul-One," I replied as I tried to force the food down my throat. Mick and I glanced at each other while he chomped another massive bite, knowing that would be the last he'd get for a while. We both wrapped up our sandwiches haphazardly and tossed them back into the fridge blindly as the radio mic crackled again.

"Thirty-One-Paul-One...seven hundred block of Nightingale Circle, near the pond, you have an assault with injuries. RP states a female in her twenties has had her throat cut. Ambulance and medics are en route and will stage until scene is secure."

Mick and I gawked at each other; our eyes wide. "Really, Mick! You had to say something tonight, didn't you?" I shook my head, and while he knew I was teasing him, we both grew serious as the words sunk in.

"Thirty-One-Paul-One, both units will be en route. Is the vic conscious?" I didn't want to ask if the victim was dead, although by asking if she were conscious, I was kinda doing just that. We stepped out of the station door with purpose. Not running, but not walking slowly either; our faces were serious as we listened to what information would come next.

"Thirty-One units, victim is in and out of consciousness and unable to talk," relayed our lifeline to the scene.

Of course, she is unable to talk—her throat is slashed, I thought as I jumped into my truck. I reached to my side, flipped off my belt radio, and grabbed my seatbelt, pulling it across my chest and reaching for the mobile radio in the car at the same time.

"Thirty-One-Paul-One, who is the RP, and does he know who the vic is or where the actor is?" I asked clearly into the mic as I reached over with my left hand and put the truck into drive.

"Thirty-One-Paul-One, the RP is a Steven Samuels who lives on Nightingale Circle. RP states he was walking his dog when he came upon the victim. RP does not know the victim, but says she looks familiar and he did not see anyone else in the area."

"Thirty-One-Paul-One, copy. Advise Adam-One please." Adam-One was my chief, who would be at home, probably just slipping into his deep sleep pattern. *Well, sorry, dude, but it's time for you to get the hell up.*

"Thirty-One-Paul-One, okay on Adam-One," the dispatcher calmly responded. I loved our dispatchers. Well, most of them, some of them were dicks. They were our eyes and ears to the incidents we were sent to. Even if they couldn't see what was happening at the scene, they obtained as much information as they could for us, so that we weren't going in as blind as we would be without them. They answered the questions as best they could so that we could decide how we should approach a scene. They kept us calm when we needed it most. Right now, the strong female voice on the other end was a lifeline to focus the adrenaline that was jetting through my veins.

I flipped on my lights and siren as I pulled out of the driveway, turning left and trying to decide which road would get me to the scene the quickest. Mick pulled out right behind me to follow my lead.

Our township was large, with mostly residential areas and horse farms. We had our areas of poverty, but it was mostly middle-class suburban neighborhoods. There were few streetlights in our town-ship and no traffic lights at all. We were considered country, even though we bordered the only city in our county. I stepped firmly on the gas pedal and slowed only long enough to make the left turn onto Hidden Valley Road. I didn't need to flip my truck. My chief would have my ass if I did. The flashing LEDs on my vehicle lit up the night like a rock concert, reflecting off the windows of the homes and the street signs we sped past.

We raced to the scene with speeds of over sixty miles per hour on backcountry roads. Not really smart, because deer and other country critters would often find themselves as part of the pavement after they left the wooded areas and wandered into the street. Quietly to myself, I prayed to God that He kept those critters safe on the side of the road, and not make me have to choose between slamming on my brakes to avoid them or taking their lives. It didn't matter if it was a squirrel or a person, I didn't want to end a living creature's life.

When we grew closer to the area, we turned our sirens and lights off. As we slowed, we cracked open our windows and began doing what we were trained for. We searched visually and listened to the sounds of the night. Somewhere out here was a bad guy, someone who hurt a person. Someone who had left a girl with her throat slashed on the side of the road. There was a bend ahead of me and I knew the pond was on the right side after I negotiated the curve. Mick and I both slowed down to almost a crawl as we came out of the bend.

A man wearing khaki pants, a blue jacket, and white shirt stood in front of us holding a leash that was attached to a small brown mutt in his arms. He looked pale in my headlights, most likely a result of what he'd seen. I examined the caller quickly—no blood on him, not even on his hands. He wasn't going to be my first suspect.

"Thirty-One-Paul-One, both units are on-scene," I called out on the mobile radio as I put my truck in park. Before I opened my door, I took one more scan over the area, glancing in the shadows to see if we would be in danger after we exited our vehicles. There was nothing in sight, so I opened the truck door as Mick opened his door behind me. I looked left, while he looked right, searching the woods again. Nothing.

Briefly, in the back of my mind, I took in the scents of the night. There was the smell of jasmine...the earthy scent of the woods...the smell of the stale water in the pond. But there was something else there...something that smelled of leather and death. A shiver tore down my spine, but I brushed the thought and feeling aside.

We took off running toward the victim and I pulled gloves out of my back pocket as I approached her. Protection from biohazards was ingrained in my head. I don't care who you are or how healthy you might be, if there were body fluids around, I wore protection, plain and simple.

As I pulled my second glove on, I was close enough to see details of the young woman lying on the ground. She wasn't moving, but she could be unconscious right now. I grabbed my lapel mic and barked out, "Thirty-One-Paul-One, scene secure, send EMS in *now!*"

"Thirty-One-Paul-One, scene secure, EMS will proceed in," the firm voice repeated on my chest microphone.

"Son of a bitch," I said as I dropped to my knees and put both my hands on the front of the girl's gaping throat. "Shit!" Muscle and tissue were ripped aside; blood ran down the pale skin of her neck as her heart continued to pump, slowly, much too slowly. We were going to lose her soon.

When my hands touched her neck, her eyes fluttered slowly and finally opened. She stared at me for a long moment before a raspy sound escaped from her throat. I think she meant to scream, but all that came out was a strangled hiss.

"It's okay, it's okay. Help is on the way." Jesus, I had never seen anything like this. Never in my years out here—in all my training classes, in all the horrible videos we watched—had I seen anything like this, *ever*. Then it hit me as I stared down at the victim. I knew her. Just then, Mick came around my other side and saw her.

"Shit, Kris...that's Dawn." His eyes were wide, and his voice an octave higher with surprise. Yeah, we knew her. We had arrested her a couple of years ago when we found her and a couple of her friends smoking marijuana in the park. I remember taking her home that night and feeling for her when I walked out of the house and could still hear her parents chewing her out in the kitchen after I told them what had happened.

Dawn looked at me, trying hard to say something. She grabbed on to my arm with the little strength that she had left. "Heeeeeee," was all she got out.

"He what, Dawn? Who did this to you?" I needed to find out more before we lost her again to the blackness. I tried to speak as calmly as I could, but with the adrenaline rushing through my system, it was difficult.

She blinked hard, trying to focus on me and hissed out, "Heeee bit meeee." Her soft brown eyes began to lose focus; her pupils dilated as I watched from above, powerless to do anything for her.

Mick and I shared a look of confusion. *Did she really just say that?* The question was evident in both sets of our eyes. "Dawn, did you say someone bit you or hit you?"

For one small moment, I felt her hand squeeze my arm with the last ounce of her strength, and then her fingers released my arm and fell to the ground with a soft thud. I would never have my answer. Mick and I watched as the life flowed out of her. In that brief moment, time stopped, and all was silent. It was as though I had been listening to her heartbeat, one, two, three times, and then it was no more.

Then just as suddenly, it was as if someone hit the volume button again, and the EMS and medics arrived and pushed Mick and me out of the way. We stood off to the side and observed as they tried to bring life back to this twenty-year-old woman. *Damn...damn...damn!* I clamped my eyes shut, took a deep breath, and yanked off my gloves as fast as I could, throwing them onto the ground in the growing pile of medical debris that was being used on her. It wouldn't matter. No matter what they did, she was gone. I couldn't hear her heart beating anymore. Wait—I couldn't hear her heartbeat even when it was beating...or could I? I shook my head to clear it. I was either more tired than I realized, or I was losing it.

The activity around me brought me back to the present. It was like a carnival with all of the lights flashing and a siren in the distance moving closer. I turned back to the medical workers; they were slowing up on what they were doing. I heard a medic say, "We need to call her. There's nothing else we can do."

"Shit…shit…shit…." With my hands resting on my hips over my duty belt, I sighed. I forced myself to take a cleansing breath and froze. Wait. That smell, the smell of leather and death…I could smell it again. I tilted my nose up in the air and sniffed. Faint, but distinct. I glanced over my shoulder at the victim; she was wearing jeans and a light green sweater, no leather. The smell of death had yet to descend on her, although the coppery scent of blood was strong in the air.

I closed my eyes and sniffed again, turning in a slow circle, allowing the breeze to filter over me. I faced in the direction of the breeze and caught the scent again. It drew a chill over me from deep inside. Somewhere in the deep recesses of my mind, I recognized it. I stared into the darkness of the woods beyond the water. The feeling that I was being watched was strong, heated, but that could have easily come from one of the ten or so people milling around me.

"Kris…hey, Kris…" Mick was trying to get my attention. I dismissed the woods and focused on him. "Chief wants you to answer your phone." I hadn't even heard it going off. I removed it from my belt, woke it up and redialed his number.

"Yeah, Chief, I'm here," I said when he answered.

"Kris, why didn't you answer your phone?" He sounded tense and tired.

"Cuz, I'm a little busy here, Chief," I retorted before I took a breath and continued as I turned my back on the scene and walked away. "Twenty-year-old female with a large neck wound. She didn't make it. It doesn't look like a knife wound—I've never seen anything like it before." Not sure why I told him all this, because I was pretty sure Mick had already filled him in.

"Whatcha gonna do now?" he asked me.

"Tape up and start the process. I'll notify the county detectives, ask them to send the team out. I'll take up with the team when they arrive. I think the medics have already made notification to the coroner." I paused. "Did Mick tell you who it was?" I was walking back to my truck now, anxious to get the scene under control and set up the tape to keep as much integrity to the area as I could.

"No, he didn't. Who was it?" the Chief asked quietly.

"Dawn, Dawn Taylor," I said delicately.

"Ah, shit…." The Chief sighed loudly into my ear. We all knew the Taylors, and not just because we had arrested the daughter, but also because Mark Taylor was one of the township supervisors, and a real pain in the ass when it came to our department. "Once you have the scene secured, Kris, have Mick and someone else hold the perimeter and go make the notification."

Damn it! "Can't Mick do the notification?" I asked tensely, already knowing the answer to that. I hated notifications, seriously hated them, with a fucking passion. "I don't want to leave the scene before the detectives are here," I added, hoping it would sway him from what he wanted me to do.

"No, I know you don't like them, Kris, but you know the Taylors better than he does, and besides, you are more sensitive when it comes to these things." It's always nice to know your chief thinks you do a good job, but I really wished I sucked at this particular task.

"He knows how to be sensitive, you know," I bit back. I almost added, you could come out and give it, but I knew better.

"Kris, just go do it. Get it over with, then give me a call and let me know how it went." Yeah, like it could go over any other way than horrible. I groaned as I reached into the back of my truck and grabbed the large roll of crime scene tape.

"Fine," I muttered before I put my phone away.

"Hey, Mick," I called to get his attention. "Get someone to help you put this up." I handed him the spool of yellow crime scene tape. "I want it three hundred yards all the way around the scene. Use the natural border of the water on that side over there." I pointed to where I wanted the tape as we spoke.

"Get EMS to move their vehicles and gear out of the scene. They can clear since the coroner will be taking care of the body." The body, not fifteen minutes dead, and now it was just a body. I shook my head.

"Then talk to the witness and get his statement." I was approaching Mick as I spoke, talking quieter as I got closer to him.

"Kris, you ever see anything like that before? I mean, damn—her throat was like gone. Do you think an animal did that? She said someone bit her, didn't she?" His eyes looked spooked and wild.

"Mick, I don't know what the hell did that—and no, I have never seen anything like it." But as I said that, I felt as if I might be lying. Had I ever seen anything like that? I shook away the question and continued. "Let's hope we never see anything like it again. Look, I have to give notification." He visibly cringed. He knew my feelings on them. "Chief wants you to make sure the scene is secure and get the witness statement. Have the fire department close off the roadway to keep the looky-lous out of here, only residents should access the road. I'll be back as soon as I can."

Mick grabbed my arm before I turned away. "You gonna be okay doing that?"

"Yeah, I'll be fine." *I hope*, I said to myself. I walked away, stopping to talk to a couple of people on my way, passing along instructions as I went.

Once back in my truck, I called the dispatcher on my cellphone, telling her to contact the detectives and the CSI team and have them respond. I gave her a little bit more information to pass along and told her I would be en route to 435 Valley Spring Road for the notification. After she wished me luck, I hung up and put the car in gear.

I've been lucky for the last two years to have been spared giving any notifications. Most death notifications had come when I was off duty, or my partner took them for me. Flashes of my past swept through my mind and my palms began to sweat.

CHAPTER FOUR

JULIAN

*J*leaned on the wall outside Alexander's office and put my head back against the drywall. I had to let go of the anger I had for him. I knew he wanted the same thing I did. He wanted revenge on Damon. He'd loved Calista as much as I had, maybe more, but I'd been the lucky one—the one she had chosen to mate with. Well, maybe chosen wasn't the right word for it. Just thinking of her made my heart ache. I shook it to clear the memories; memories would not help me focus.

I had been waiting for another chance to find Damon. It had been years since he had last shown his display of inhumanity toward our race, his race. Some people speculated that since the killings had stopped, maybe Damon had somehow been killed.

But in my soul, I knew that wasn't true. I knew that if he were truly dead, I would have felt it. I knew Damon better than anyone. He was a part of me—a very sad, sinister, twisted part of me.

I shook my head as I walked down the beige-carpeted hallway and toward the elevator. Doors lined the hall on both sides, and most were closed. Since it was late, almost six in the morning, most people had already gone home for the day—at least, those who worked on this floor had.

The company was called Virtual Military Force Security or VMF for short. To most people, it was your run of the mill security company dealing with home and personal security issues. On the floors below, there was activity twenty-four hours a day. It was only up here on the third floor where the night people worked: my people, the vampires.

Up here, the VMF stood for Vampire Military Force, and while we did the same things as those on the floors below, we also policed our own breed. We were the enforcers charged with keeping the vampires in line. Agents like me traveled the country to protect our own and the humans from the vampires that had gotten out of hand.

Master Alexander was our boss. He was in charge of making sure our race was kept quiet and survived. He made the decisions as to what punishment would be dealt out and which enforcers would search for the wild vampires. He was the one to make the ultimate decision as to whether they would live, or die forever.

I had worked for the VMF since I was first turned. It had been sixty-five years since I joined this race. My father had turned me when I was thirty-six human years old. To any human, I looked to be that age; to our kind, I was now over a hundred.

I had been raised with the knowledge that, one day, I would be turned, and that I would follow in my father's footsteps to work for the VMF. He was one of the founding fathers of the company. He was four hundred and sixty-seven in vampire years and had only recently decided to leave the field and "retire," as the humans called it.

By all rights, I could have held the position Alex did, but I always felt that my place was out in the field, not behind a desk giving orders. Alex's pompous attitude fit more into that mold.

When I entered the lobby, I found Gabriel sitting in a chair, tapping his foot to some beat in his head. Probably some silly country tune he had last heard. He grinned and stood up quickly.

"I hear we're going hunting!" He clapped me on the back, still grinning like a schoolboy.

It was hard not to get caught up in his carefree attitude. He was a big guy who looked menacing until he started belting out a Garth

Brooks song, then he looked like a silly, overgrown kid of twenty-five. I pushed the down button next to the elevator door.

Gabriel had been turned young. His sire had been a woman who wanted the taste of him too badly to wait until he fully matured. Our maturity age was normally between thirty and forty, and that is the best time for us to change. It is a time when we can look younger or older as we need to. Serena, Gabe's maker, had liked them young, and she had been punished for this deed. She no longer walked the earth now; Alex and I had seen to that. Gabe knew this and understood, so there was no animosity from him that we had removed her.

"Yep, looks like it," I responded, trying to return his jovial attitude. He was taller than I was, by about eight inches. With his dark brown hair kept military short, he had a smile that I knew melted women's hearts, and a sensitivity that was rare for our breed. He was a true ladies' man: gentle and caring. But get him in the battle zone and he was a force to be reckoned with.

"When are we leaving, and where are we going?" asked Gabe, almost bouncing on his toes.

Gabe was like a son to me at times, and at others, he was my confidant. While I wanted to do this job on my own, there was no one else I would've wanted with me if I had to take someone. I smirked as I took in his scuffed cowboy boots as the elevator door slid open.

"A small place out in the countryside of Pennsylvania, west of Philadelphia. We're leaving at sunset," I responded as we entered the small metal box. "I've been there before. It's actually a pretty nice area." *With a lot of heart wrenching memories*, I thought.

"Any good places to see the ladies?" he grinned as he asked.

I laughed. "Not sure, been a long time since I was in that area." *Thirty-five years, to be exact.* "We'll see what entertainment we can find for you after we get set up and start looking around. Maybe all your sweetness with the ladies can help us get some info on what's happening in the area."

"Awesome! I love working with the ladies," he replied as we stepped off the elevator in the basement parking lot. "Hey, two questions. First, you want me to drive? And who're we hunting for this time?"

I stopped abruptly and took a deep breath before I turned to look at him. "Damon." His eyes flashed wide. "And I'll drive. We're taking the 'Stang." His jaw dropped.

"Wow," was the only word to leave his lips before I turned and went off toward my truck. As I climbed inside, I heard Gabe mumble, "Oh man, this is gonna be interesting—Damon and the 'Stang…holy shit."

I called over my shoulder, "Be ready at sunset. I'll pick you up." I closed the door to my F-150 and cranked over the engine.

One of my favorite CDs began to play and I got lost in the haunting melody of *Evanescence*. My mind wandered as I drove, and for the first time in a long while, I allowed myself to think about Calista, revisiting the very first night that I had met her.

Back then, Alex and I were partners; he wasn't the head of the VMF yet. We were on a job and in search of two vampires who had run amok and brought too much attention to our kind. Those who did not abide by our laws were removed. Not only removed from the public, but from the population, period. We had started a search as soon as we heard they were getting a bit too out of hand, robbing people. It wasn't only that they were stealing from people forcefully; they were doing it in vampire mode. They weren't using weapons, but their unusual strength, speed, and a couple pairs of canine teeth that were way too noticeable.

It was our job to find them and make them disappear, forever.

We had heard that they were in this area, and Alex made some phone calls, one of them being to a woman named Calista. He'd known her for a while and had a budding relationship that he entertained when he was in the area. He had talked about her many times, and there always seemed to be a bit of yearning in his voice. I wondered if the feelings he had were more one-sided than he said they were. He recently told me that he thought she was going to be the one to mate with. I knew that was a hard decision for him, especially since he would soon lead the force.

We were to meet her and a friend at a restaurant called Night Crawlers, a place that was well known for vampire and human customers alike. I had heard of it, but had never been there.

As we walked into the establishment, our eyes scanned readily, making sure that our targets weren't there before we could relax and enjoy our visit. If they had been there, it would have been too easy. It was dark inside the bar, but our eyes were better in the dark. Alex, who stood several inches over me, found who he was looking for and walked off toward the bar.

I noticed the two women sitting on stools at the bar with two empty seats on either side of them. Both of them had long hair, one brunette and one with a beautiful shade of strawberry blond. That would be Calista. I remembered Alex saying she had beautiful hair. The brunette noticed us as we approached. She had deep brown eyes that appeared too eager, too hard for my taste. She watched us approach and I saw her quickly pass over Alex and then study me. She smiled shyly before she flicked her attention back to Alex as he stepped behind the other woman.

The brunette said something that made the other woman laugh. It was like music and my lips curled up at the sound of it. It was a solid, heartfelt laugh that sounded as if it came from her soul, and she turned in her seat to face Alex. I stood transfixed on her profile and stared as she stood and smiled up into his face. He bent to place a kiss on her lips, but she turned her head slightly and it landed on her cheek. Her eyes were closed as they turned in my direction.

"Hello, Alex. It's always good to see you again," she said, just loudly enough for me to hear it. It reached my ears, mellow and strong.

"Hello, my dear," he responded softly. He put his arm around her shoulders as he smiled at her friend and said, "Hey there, Gina Marie, how are you?" The tone of his voice made me think there was no love lost between them and he was acknowledging her only out of respect.

He didn't wait for an answer, but turned around so that he faced me, and introduced me to Calista.

"Calista, dear, this is my best friend, Julian," he said cheerfully, proud to be displaying her on his arm.

I noticed the stiffening of her spine as he spoke and wondered if she didn't care for the endearment that he used. She was looking down at the floor and started trailing her gaze up my body from my feet, taking in my black work boots, and slowly working her way up my jean-clad legs. As soon as her eyes touched me, I felt my body warm. I felt the heat building inside the very core of my soul. It felt as if she was physically touching me, like her hands were trailing up my body instead of her eyes. By the time she got to my waist, I felt myself starting to get hard and I was dying to see what was in her eyes. She made her way up, inch by slow inch, and I felt my heart skip a beat as I held my breath. Her gaze reached my stomach and chest. She paused at my neck, watching the vein tick in the side. I saw her gently lift her chin and take a small sniff of the air. As soon as my scent hit her nose, her eyes flashed to mine, locking instantly.

An electric shock ran through my body and I couldn't move. Her eyes were green, a deep, intense green, and then all of a sudden, they weren't. They changed to gray before finally turning a vivid blue. They were wide as she regarded me, and she whispered, "Jewels."

I still couldn't move. I continued to stare into her eyes. I didn't speak—it was as if my tongue was stuck to the roof of my mouth. For a few more seconds, we studied one another, and I felt the electricity speeding through my body, touching every nerve and making every nerve ending tingle.

Finally, Alex broke the stare by saying, "How did you know we call him Jules?" He bent over to see into her face, but she was looking past him, keeping her vision locked on mine.

She seemed to shake her head to clear it and turned to face Alex. "I didn't know that was his nickname. I think his eyes look like jewels, dark sapphires on the outside and rich aquamarines on the inside." She gave him a small smile before peering at me again, and then turned to look away. I watched her take a deep breath, shaking her head again.

Her voice sounded strained as she spoke. "It's nice to finally meet you, Julian. Alex has mentioned you quite a bit." She smiled but didn't meet my eyes again.

"Same here, Calista. It's a pleasure to meet you, too." I refrained from offering her my hand. If just our eyes connecting could be so strong, I didn't think I could handle touching her without dragging her body to mine and kissing every inch of it that I could reach.

I did, however, shake her friend's hand as introductions were made. Gina Marie offered a smile that made me think she knew exactly what had just transpired between Calista and me. Which I found totally strange, because I had no idea what had just happened.

For the next two hours, Gina Marie and I sat and talked. I kept my back to Alex and Calista and enjoyed the conversation that we were having. Gina Marie was smart and intense and had a great sense of humor. Even though it was easy to talk to her, I could feel Calista seated behind me. Her scent swirled around my head, filing my senses and making me dizzy.

She was getting close to mating time, I could sense it—for some reason, all I could think about was how I wanted to be the one to mate with her. I wanted to watch my child grow within her. The process would finish turning her and once that was done, we could live our lives together, forever.

What the hell was I thinking? She was with Alex. Alex wanted her for that. At least, Alex wanted to mate with her—I don't know if he ever thought about anything else for the future, but he at least wanted to carry on the bloodline. I couldn't do that to him, he was my best friend. Besides, the thought of mating with anyone had always been the last of my thoughts.

Yet, as I sat talking with Gina Marie, I could not help but listen to the cadence of Calista's voice behind me and wish it were me sitting face to face with her.

By the time the night was over, it was all I could do not to throw her over my shoulder and walk out the door. What would she do if I did? What would she think? Did I even care what she thought? I wanted her and that was all I knew.

I watched Alex walk away to speak to someone he knew and intended to follow him. But I climbed off of my bar stool just as Calista did, and we bumped shoulders. An intense wave of heat passed through my body and I gasped.

We turned to face one another, meaning only to say a polite goodbye. We were eye to eye, almost exactly the same height. She was so close; I could smell her without trying. The current was soaring through me and she parted her lips, never taking her gaze from mine.

"Jewels," she said so quietly I could barely hear her over the noise of the bar. She looked at my lips and I had the urge to move closer and touch mine to hers. She flicked her gaze back to mine. "The two stones that are within my soul, sapphires for the dark of the sky and aquamarines for my dreams of the beautiful blue oceans in the heat of the summer."

I was unable to look away from the liquid blue color of her irises. They were so bright and warm that they called out for me to fall into them. "Calista...you don't know how much I want to take you in my arms right now and run away with you." The words fell off my tongue before I could even contemplate saying them.

Her eyes widened and a sly smile crept along her face. "Then let's run," she said.

CHAPTER FIVE

KRISTIN

I groaned as I put the truck in gear and started heading to the Taylor residence.

Notifications...Fuck! I dreaded them more than anything, now more than ever. It was never easy telling someone that a loved one had died in an accident or by suicide. It was even worse to tell them someone had been murdered. I exhaled loudly. As I drove the few miles to the Taylors' home, I thought back to the time when I had been on the receiving end of the notification.

I'd worked day shift and gotten off a couple hours early. I smiled as I jumped into my Jeep and started home. It was gonna be a good night! I was determined to make it a good night. I turned up the radio, rolled down the windows, and opened the sunroof.

On my way home, I stopped at the grocery store to pick up steaks, fresh baked sourdough bread, salad fixings, and one of our favorite pasta salads that the deli had already made. I also ran into the liquor store and grabbed a bottle of white merlot. Tonight was to be a celebration.

Seven years.

We had been married for seven years now, and while I deeply loved Trevor, I had always felt that something was missing. There was nothing lacking in our relationship that I could tell. We were good friends, and even better lovers. It just felt like something had always been absent, and I figured that was just because of me.

I had met Trevor when I was in the Academy and started to do ride-alongs with the department. He had been the one to take me along. We'd become friends right from the start, and it quickly grew into more.

When the time came for him to move on to a different department, I was hired to take his old position. This was good. Working the same job, but in totally different places, worked well. We knew what the other was doing, but then again—we didn't. Working side by side would have created problems. That overbearing sense of male testosterone and protection would've gotten under my skin really quick. A year after we met, we were married and moved into our home; the one I still lived in.

When I arrived at the house, our four-legged child, Garda, a 125-pound Shiloh Shepherd, greeted me. Years before, we decided that with our jobs and the importance of them, we didn't want to have any children for a while, so we agreed to get a dog instead. It was great for us and we loved Garda. Although, I knew my biological clock was starting to tick, actually quite loudly. Maybe we could start talking about it. Maybe tonight, I would bring it up.

I put the groceries away in the fridge and went to the bedroom to change clothes, with Garda following right on my heels. Since I had not let him out as soon as I got home, he knew what was coming, and his eager eyes followed every move I made. I grabbed a pair of black running shorts and a matching black and fuchsia sports tank, while Garda entered my closet and brought over my running shoes. I chuckled and rubbed his head for a moment before pulling them on.

We jumped into my Jeep and took off for the park. While I was not one to be afraid, I always felt safer running in the local park, because I knew others would be there at this time of day. It was kind of hard to carry my off-duty gun when I was running.

The weather was perfect. It was the end of summer and the temperatures were still very warm. Garda and I got in a nice solid two-mile run and headed back home. With a quick glance at my watch, I realized I had enough time to do a quick weight workout in the basement and cranked up the music to keep me in the mood. Garda curled up outside the door to my gym, knowing better than to be underfoot as I tossed dumbbells around. He kept his eye on me, as if he were my coach, barking every once in a while as I struggled with a weight, encouraging me to finish through.

I was stronger than most women my size and age. There weren't too many women I knew who could bench press 250 pounds and not look like the Incredible Hulk. I never really told people how strong I was; even Trevor didn't know. I never could understand it, but I liked knowing that I was that powerful and that it was a secret. For some reason, the fact that it was a secret seemed normal to me.

After my workout, my legs were tired, and my arms felt like jelly. In my eyes, that was what made a workout good. In the shower, I grabbed my favorite bottle of body wash, chocolate fudge scented. Yes, I wanted to be good enough to eat tonight. I grinned and could already feel the warmth spreading within the core of my body as I imagined what would come later.

Our sex life was wonderful; never the same thing twice, never boring, always satisfying. I smiled again and belted out the words of the music playing, "It's gonna be a good night." I laughed and jumped out of the shower. After I took the blow dryer to warm up the mirror and remove steam off the glass, I took a minute to examine myself.

My body was solid and smooth. While I wasn't muscle-bound, it was obvious that I lifted, and my muscles were toned and strong. My shoulders were wide from years of swimming and lifting, and at thirty-two, my body held its hourglass figure nicely, while still allowing me to enjoy all the junk food I wanted.

My neck was long and thin and very visible, as I had short hair. My hair had been short ever since I was in the Academy when I chopped off fourteen inches. I didn't want to bother with having to pull it up every day on the job. Sometimes I missed having long hair, but mostly I was glad that it was short and easy to do. I wasn't the type to worry about my appearance, and the faster I could get done in the bathroom, the better.

My strawberry blond hair was something people had always complimented me on ever since I was a child. When I was young, I hated it, just because people would remark on it. As I grew older, I realized how much people paid to get this color, and I learned to be thankful that I had such a rare and beautiful color naturally.

My face was nothing special to me; it was just average. There was nothing too big or too small, no real prominent features, except for my eyes. My eyes...what color were they today...green. Yes, today they would be green. My eyes changed with my moods: sometimes green, sometimes blue, and when I was angry, they turned gray. I had been told they were called "mirror eyes," because they reflected my inner feelings. They were also very light-sensitive, and I wore dark shades whenever I was outside. Even when it was hazy, you'd find me hiding behind my Oakleys.

Today, the green showed my excitement at being home waiting for Trevor, the anticipation I felt when I knew we would see each other, and we would make love. Green...yes, they were green tonight for the passion that would come.

I quickly did my hair, threw on a silk button-down blouse in peach, and a pair of jeans. I went out to the kitchen barefoot and fed Garda. It was time to get dinner ready and the table set for a romantic setting. I blew out the match after I lit the last candle and heard a car pull up the drive to my house. A thrill raced through me and I figured Trevor had arrived home, but as I reached out with my hearing, I noticed that the vehicle sounded different from his compact car.

Cars didn't normally pull up to our house. We lived a quarter-mile back from the roadway, so we never saw random vehicles. That was when the first threads of something being wrong hit me. Who could be here right now? No one ever showed up at our house unless they told us they were coming. I grabbed my cellphone, which was lying on the counter where I'd tossed it after my run and looked to see if someone sent a text message saying they were stopping over. No text message, but I had eight missed calls and no messages. Another finger of dread curled around my spine.

Before I checked to see who called, I walked to the front door and peered out the small glass window. It had gotten dark while I was getting dinner ready and, from the door, I could just make out a light-colored car in the driveway. I flipped on the outside light as I opened the door. Through the glass storm door, I caught the reflective blue and gold decal on the side of the patrol car that read: "Orchard Valley Township." I looked over the hood to see a man standing on the other side...Brett, my husband's partner.

My heart stopped beating and sank. No more threads, just full-out ropes of panic and pain coursed through my body.

Okay, maybe not a good time to be bringing up this memory, I thought as I pulled up in front of the Taylors' residence. I closed my eyes and tried to compose myself. With one last deep breath, I pushed open the door and stepped down onto the driveway. There were lights on in the downstairs windows, and a woman's face pushed up to the glass in what was probably the living room. She was watching me. No turning back now. I inhaled deeply and walked up to the door, head held high, heart racing, hands shaking, and trying to remember to breathe.

CHAPTER SIX

JULIAN

*W*hen I arrived home, I was wired from the memory of first meeting Calista. All the memories seemed to have come back to life with a vengeance the moment Damon was mentioned. I wandered around my loft apartment, trying to figure out what I needed to take with me on the trip. What tools, what equipment, what weapons I needed to bring.

As I gathered my things, memories of Calista once again drifted into my mind.

"I'm not joking," I'd told her as we stood toe to toe in the bar.

"Me either." She peeked at my lips again. "Meet me here tomorrow night. I need to see you again," she rattled off quickly.

I felt the electric current run through me every time she looked at me. With her this close, I felt her energy flowing over me. She smelled so fresh, so sweet, that I wanted to close my eyes and inhale her, but I was afraid that if I did, she would be gone when I reopened them.

I glanced over her shoulder and saw Alex still talking to someone. He had his back to us, totally unaware of what was happening. I couldn't help myself; I reached up and touched the side of her face with my fingertips. Heat at hot as lava ran through my fingers into my heart. She closed her eyes, inhaling sharply as I caressed her skin.

She placed her hand on my chest right where my heart beat. Holy shit...I thought I would explode into a ball of flames. I couldn't breathe. I wanted so badly to kiss her, taste her, drown in her, and I would have if Gina Marie hadn't raised her voice to ask Alex a question about the bar tab. He had turned around and was on his way back to us. I took a step back and peeked over at Gina Marie. She winked, and I gave her a weak smile. She had watched the whole thing and looked happy about what she had seen as she chuckled.

I put my back to them as Alex returned to our group. I needed all my concentration to regain my composure. "You ready to go, Jules?" he called over Calista's head. I turned back around just in time to watch him take hold of her hands. "Goodbye, dear." He leaned in for a kiss and seemed disappointed when she gave him only a slight peck. Of course, I was thankful that I didn't have to witness a passionate goodbye between them. "We should be in the area for a while, so I will see you again soon." He kissed her forehead before turning to Gina Marie and tossing out, "See you around."

He passed by me and I took one more long look at her. She mouthed, "Tomorrow—here." I could only nod and followed Alex out of the bar. As I reached the door, I could still hear Gina Marie laughing.

The rest of that night and the entire next day, I could think of nothing but her. Even as I closed my eyes during the hours of the sun, I could not get her off my mind. It was impossible to sleep without her entering my dreams. It was as if my life had not started until the very moment that I saw her, and I would never be able to live without having her as mine.

Time was ticking slower than ever and I wondered how I could get away from Alex long enough to see her. As fate would have it, Alex told me he had a source that wanted to speak with him, and he had to go alone. He said that he was going to meet up with some other friends in the area afterward and asked if I wanted to join him later. I begged off quickly.

Just like that, my night was free. I should have felt guilty meeting Calista behind Alex's back, but I couldn't dredge up the feeling. All I thought about was that she was meant to be mine. There had not been a woman in my life for years. Not since I had last sired a child with someone. I had not wanted anyone in my life since then, but all of a sudden, I had to have it, had to have her.

When I knew Alex was gone, I dressed in my black boots, jeans, a long-sleeved burgundy V-neck sweater, and my leather jacket, and headed down to the garage of the company-owned house where we were staying. There were several cars kept in the garage, and I knew exactly which one I wanted to drive. I walked purposely past several not-so-special traditional cars and stopped in front of the brand-new midnight-blue Mustang and grinned.

I pulled up in front of Night Crawlers with my heart pounding. Before I could turn the car off, the passenger door opened, and Calista climbed inside quickly.

Jesus, I hadn't dreamed it; she was more beautiful than I remembered. I stared at her while she pulled the door shut and turned to me. Her eyes met mine and I knew she felt the same way I did. She wore jeans and a dark purple blouse; her hair hung around her face, waving gently from her movement.

"Where's Alex?" she asked quietly.

"Out working a case, then going out with friends," I replied, never taking my eyes off hers. Her eyes narrowed, turning slightly gray before opening back up in a bright green color.

"Let's go back to the VMF house," she stated clearly.

So she knew about the VMF? How much had Alex told her? I reached across the seat and pushed a lock of strawberry blond hair off her shoulder. Silk, it felt like silk. I glanced at her face once before putting the car in gear.

As we started the ride back to the house, she put her left hand on my thigh. The muscles bunched under the slight pressure, but slowly relaxed. For the entire ride, she sang to the music on the radio, her right arm hanging out of the window and her left hand resting gently on my thigh. I kept quiet and tried to memorize every moment of our time together.

When we pulled up to the house, she climbed out and stood looking up at the sky. "The sky right now is like your eyes. The deep dark sapphire of night glistening with stars."

I stood behind her. "No one has ever put it that way," I said softly.

"That's what I thought when I saw them last night. Now that I've seen the sky here, I know that I was correct. The depths of your eyes are like looking into the galaxy." She was still staring into the sky, her back to me.

I couldn't resist any longer—I reached out to touch her just as she turned *to face me. We were eye to eye again, neither of us breathing. My hand cupped her cheek, my thumb slid over her open lips, and I pulled her to me slowly.*

When our lips met, it was as if the galaxy above swallowed us in an explosion of the sun. The moment our lips touched, I no longer knew where I stopped, and she began. We seemed to have melted together, to have become one in that first kiss.

Her hands gripped my shirt, pulling me closer. My other arm wrapped around her body and I held her against me. We clung to each other tighter than I could have ever thought possible, the kiss so deep it was as if we could've existed with one heart beating.

She strained hard against me, as if trying to get inside of me. She slowly ground against me, her hips making contact with the erection that was begging for freedom. I moaned deep in my throat and pushed myself as firmly as I could against her while standing up.

Holy shit, I was gonna explode here in the driveway, right here under the stars. I wanted her—right that moment I needed her more than I needed air, blood, a heartbeat. I needed her and I had to be inside her, feel her warmth wrapped around me, explode within her, make her mine—forever.

I pushed her against the side of the Mustang roughly. She gasped as I put my hands under her ass and lifted her onto the hood. Her legs wrapped around my waist, the perfect height to push against the length of me, and she tried to shove my jacket off my shoulders. I moaned again into her mouth and felt my teeth begin to extend as I shrugged the jacket off one shoulder and then the other.

My hands kneaded her ass for a moment before moving to her waist. One of my hands stayed there, while the other followed the line of her waistband to the front. I released the button on her jeans and quickly unzipped them. This was not going to be a slow loving union; this was going to be hard and fast. She moaned into my mouth and put her hands up to my neck, pulling me closer, deepening the kiss, if that was even possible. Our tongues probed with need and pure lust. My fangs lengthened completely, and her tongue rubbed over them carefully.

I unbuttoned her blouse from the bottom, the first two buttons slowly, but then my fingers shook, and I finished as quickly as I could. She leaned her body back to allow me to work, and brought her own hands to my waistband, untucking the end of my shirt. Her hands grazed my skin and felt like fire against it. I felt dizzy and strained against her as hard as I could, briefly wondering if I was hurting her. She broke the kiss only long enough to pull my shirt over my head, her mouth immediately reconnecting with mine.

I cradled her face and pulled back; her eyes were dark green, the passion shining in them matched the heat of my blood. I started covering her face with kisses, licking her skin with the tip of my tongue, tasting her, being careful not to nip her with my teeth. Her pulse beat fast under my tongue as I traveled down the column of her neck. I held back from the urge to sink my canines into her sweet skin.

Her hands moved to my waistband and I felt the instant release when she unzipped my jeans and allowed my length into the fresh night air. Her hand wrapped around my shaft and I shivered. I had to have her now.

I pushed her back onto the hood and grabbed the sides of her jeans, yanking them off as she arched her back to assist me. Her eyes were half closed as she watched me. I couldn't even take the time to remove her panties. With a quick jerk, the material tore away, and a gasp fell from her lips before a naughty smile crossed her lips. I ran my hands from her knees up her thighs, her legs wrapping around my waist, opening herself to me. Her hot, wet, silky flesh called out to be touched. I took a deep breath trying to calm myself and slow down before I put my thumb on that special knot that would make her explode. She wiggled under my hand and instantly cried out as her body shook. Fuck! I almost lost it just at the sight of her climaxing.

Her breathing slowed, and her body finally stopped quivering. She opened her eyes and reached for me. I took both of her hands and pulled her to a sitting position, her legs still wrapped around me.

Somehow, she'd managed to get my pants down enough to totally free me. She clasped her arms tightly around my neck, pulling me close, and without another thought, I thrust forward and entered her.

With an intensity I had never felt before, I drove into her again and again. She called out my name as I grew closer to my climax. Her silent invitation was received when she threw her head back and exposed her throat to me. I had not taken blood from a vein in so long. While I wanted her to be mine, I hadn't intended to drink from her, not that night, not without her *permission. Yet, I could not resist the bloodlust with the sweet scent of her that hit me at that very moment and allowed my teeth to sink into the soft skin of her neck.*

A small gasp left her mouth as I sucked deeply from her throat. The blood tasted so rich and pure that it was intoxicating. She raised her head and kissed my neck twice before she bit down on me. She still had her human teeth, but the strength of her jaw allowed her to break the skin with little effort. As soon as I felt her suck deeply on my neck, I thrust once more and exploded into the deep wetness of her body. She was mine...totally and forever.

Our bodies shook as the connection began. We had mated, without talking about it, without planning it, without even knowing each other. Our blood mingled within our two bodies; the feeling of intoxication intensified, and my knees felt weak. I leaned against her, trying to catch my breath as I licked her wound. It was done. We were one.

I came back to the present and found myself lying on my bed, my dick throbbing with want behind the denim material of my jeans. *Calista...*a single tear trickled down from the corner of my eye into the temple of my hair. *I will avenge your death and then I will come to find you in the afterlife. I cannot walk one day longer without you.* I closed my eyes and eventually fell into a sleep filled with love and joy. If only they weren't just dreams...

CHAPTER SEVEN

KRISTIN

I walked up the driveway to the Taylors' residence and glanced over the front of the house to calm my racing mind. It was a beautiful two-story Colonial home painted in the traditional Williamsburg blue with black shutters. The walkway to the front porch had slabs of river rock surrounded by mulch. The gardens were perfectly tended. *Gardens that will never see grandchildren running around in them,* I thought as I stepped up to the door.

Before I could put my hand up to knock, the porch light clicked on, momentarily blinding me, and the front door opened. My eyes grew accustomed to the lighting rapidly and took in the man and woman standing before me.

Mr. Taylor appeared to be in his early forties, about six feet tall. He had an athletic build, wide shoulders, and a thin waist. His face always held the same stern look, as if he was constantly about to yell at someone to stop what they were doing. His hair was a dirty blond, cut simple, short, and parted to the side.

Mrs. Taylor stood beside him, almost as tall as her husband, with long brown hair and chocolate brown eyes. She was wearing a pair of slacks that accented her thin waist and long legs, a floral print blouse, and no shoes on her feet.

"Officer Greene," she said, "what a pleasure to see you, please come in." Mrs. Taylor smiled, but it looked strained. I had always liked her and her husband, despite the fact that he constantly looked angry, or maybe concerned was more like it. They had actually been instrumental in me getting my job out here in Fawn Hollow. She was almost maternal toward me when she spoke, which I thought odd since she looked to be only slightly older than I was. In the ten years I had worked here, she didn't seem to have aged a day. She was either blessed or had a damn good plastic surgeon.

"Mr. and Mrs. Taylor." I nodded and stepped into the foyer, swallowing down the bile that had once again risen in my throat.

Mrs. Taylor motioned for me to follow her into the living room, always the pleasant hostess. "I assume you wish to speak with Mr. Taylor about some township business." She looked over her shoulder, a perfectly manicured eyebrow raised.

I skirted her look and, instead, glanced over my shoulder at Mr. Taylor. He stood behind me, watching me intently, and I noticed he sniffed the air, almost as I had at the scene. "Actually, I need to speak to both of you," I said quietly, making eye contact with him.

Mr. Taylor's nostrils flared, and his mouth slacked open slightly. "Dead, she's dead?"

My jaw wanted to drop but somehow, I kept it in place. Damn, did I forget to wipe the sign off my face that said, 'Hey, man, sorry, but your daughter's dead'? How the hell did he know? Had someone from the scene called him already?

I turned to Mrs. Taylor and found her face contorted in horror, eyes wide, mouth open as if she would speak.

Wait, this was not going how it should. I cleared my head and glanced between them. Mr. Taylor moved to stand beside his wife, his arm wrapped around her shoulders and they both gave me their attention, waiting patiently.

"Mr. and Mrs. Taylor, I am very sorry to say that your daughter, Dawn, is dead." I hated saying that sentence, but it was a sentence that was drilled into you from the moment you entered the academy. You do not say, I'm sorry your daughter was in an accident, or your daughter did not make it. Not in the first sentence. You can elaborate later, but that first sentence had to be the one that they would remember for the rest of their lives. The one that told them, this is not a sick joke, and they are not just going to wake up tomorrow and find her asleep in her bed. That sentence had to say that it was real, and it was final.

They stared at me blankly. Mrs. Taylor's lips moved, and I could have sworn I heard her say, "He found us." I thought it was my imagination until I looked into Mr. Taylor's steel-gray eyes and saw them widen as he flicked a glance my way to see if I'd heard. I managed to keep my face perfectly clear and thought I would mull over that statement later.

Mrs. Taylor got herself back under control and seemed to go into the shock stage immediately. She sank down in a wingback chair, hands on her lap, staring at me, but not really seeing me.

I gave my attention to Mr. Taylor, who was eyeballing me critically. When I made eye contact with him, it was almost as if he was measuring me up from the inside out. The way he was able to look into my eyes was almost as if I was standing naked in front of him. I wanted to shield myself, but I stood still and silent, waiting to see what questions would come out of his mouth. There were always questions after dropping the bomb I had.

Mr. Taylor took a moment longer to appraise me before he finally asked, "How?"

So, I thought the first sentence was hard to say; the second one didn't seem any easier. I took a deep breath. "Mr. Taylor, it appears that her throat was cut." I wasn't going to tell him that it was ripped out, that muscle and tissue were torn to shreds, and that she had bled out in my hands as I watched her go.

He winced. "Cut. Are you sure, Officer Greene? Could it have been more of a rip? A tear?" he asked curtly.

I felt as though I'd been slapped with just his tone alone. I shifted my stance but kept eye contact. First of all, don't question what I say or how I say it; after ten years, I know what I'm doing. And secondly, why the hell did he even ask me that? How could he have known?

That was my initial thought when I first saw the damage, that someone had ripped open Dawn's throat—but how, I didn't even know why I thought that.

My years of professionalism stayed with me and I answered Mr. Taylor politely. "Mr. Taylor, I am unsure of the exact cause of death. It appears to be some kind of a laceration to her neck." His eyes narrowed as if he knew I was lying. "Our department, along with county detectives, will be doing a complete investigation. I would be more than happy to explain more after the autopsy is completed."

"Officer Greene, can you tell me..." He seemed to be having a hard time putting the rest of his sentence together but gathered himself and finished. "Was there a hole in her chest, above her heart?"

The tension in the room hit a new all-time high. I shifted to see that Mrs. Taylor was sitting on the edge of her seat, waiting intently for my reply.

"No, sir, there didn't seem to be one," I answered, but felt as if I should be asking a question next, like why the hell would he be asking if there was a hole in her chest.

When I finished my response, I heard Mrs. Taylor's stuttered sigh. I looked between the two of them, trying to put some pieces together. They weren't fitting.

At that moment, my cellphone rang on my belt, and I quickly apologized; I should have left it in the car. I grabbed it, meaning to turn it off and put it back on my belt, but I saw the way Mrs. Taylor was looking up at Mr. Taylor and instinct told me I should give them a second. Was that a look of hope I saw flash inside her eyes?

I turned back to Mr. Taylor. "Excuse me, sir, I need to take this." I stepped into the entranceway and bladed myself to the left so that I could see them in my peripheral vision.

I put my phone to my ear, "Go ahead, Chief," I said quietly, while still watching what was happening in the living room, without seeming obvious.

Mr. Taylor squatted down in front of Mrs. Taylor and took her hand. I almost choked on her next set of words, "I'm next, aren't I?"

What?

He glanced my way and looked back at his wife quickly, as if concerned that I might have heard what she'd said. "No, I'll call the VMF and we'll get help."

I was so intent on what was being said on the other side of the room; thank god I had been blessed with amazing hearing. Most people would have heard only soft murmurs coming from them, but I could actually make out the words. Although my hearing wasn't working very well with what was being said right into my ear, because I totally missed what my chief had just said to me. I was trying to figure out what the "VMF" was and why they would be calling them.

"Look, Chief, let me call you back in a few—I'm still at the Taylors' residence." I hung up without waiting for a response and put the phone back in my holder on my duty belt.

I returned to the living room and stood observing the Taylors as they stared at one another, not saying anything, but still appearing as if they were having a conversation.

"Mr. and Mrs. Taylor, I am so very sorry," I said quietly, falling back into my job as the person who had just given them some terrible news. "Is there anything I can do for you; anyone you would like me to call before I leave?"

"Thank you, Kristin." Mr. Taylor used my first name as he stood. I didn't mind him using it, a lot of people did. "I appreciate your assistance with this matter, but we will be fine. I assume you have things to get done." I blinked. Wow—was I just dismissed? I had never been dismissed from a notification before. It was more common that I had to look for a chance to slide out the door unnoticed as more family began to arrive and the pain of loss started to become over-whelming.

"Um…okay, yes, sir. I do need to get back to the scene. I will be in touch soon." I nodded and turned toward the door to leave.

"Kristin," Mrs. Taylor called, and I waited for her to join us in the foyer.

"Yes, Mrs. Taylor?"

"Kristin, you of all people need to be careful after this." She came to stand in front of me, and reached for one of my hands. I was a bit taken aback. I was used to people worrying about my safety in my job, but never quite to this extent.

"Me? Why me?"

She shook her head slightly and squeezed my hand once before releasing it. "Just be careful out there, okay?" She looked as if she wanted to say more but didn't.

"Of course, of course I will." I felt confused. It almost felt like a warning—but I didn't understand it. I fled the residence quickly, heading back to the protectiveness of my truck.

I had a strange sense that there was something just not right about what had occurred in there. I mean, more so not right than just a young woman being killed. There was something else going on with all of this.

Where were the tears? At most notifications, people burst into tears, or threw themselves at you begging for it not to be true. The fact that there were no tears, and no begging, was odd to say the least. It was almost as if they expected this to happen, had been waiting for it.

The investigator in me began to hum to life, the questions spinning around. Who did Mrs. Taylor think had found them? How had Mr. Taylor known she was dead and that her throat was more than just cut open with a knife? Why did he ask if there had been a hole in her chest? And who the hell was the VMF?

I rolled back up to the scene and saw that most of the medical vehicles were gone. The crime scene team had apparently just arrived, and I jumped out of the truck and walked over to Detective Davis.

"Hey, Jim, thanks for coming out." I gave him what smile I could muster. He was a mentor of sorts to me. It was my dream to be as good as he was when it came to investigating crime scenes. He taught me a lot over the last few years and there was always more to learn.

"No problem, Kris." He lifted his fancy Nikon camera from his bag and put it around his neck. "What do we know?" he asked.

"Not much, Jim." I shook my head in kind of a daze, still trying to figure out what had created the tearing in Dawn's throat. "You get a chance to look at the body yet?" I asked.

"Yeah, I did." His voice sounded flat; no emotion evident in it. "It looks similar to some pictures I have seen from a case in the next county over."

"Really?" I hadn't heard of anything like this, but then again, I refused to listen to the news or read the paper. It was too depressing.

"Yeah, they had several homicides like this about a week ago." He eyed me with raised brows. He probably thought I should have known this.

I shrugged. "I'm not too in touch with the news these days." I looked past him to where Dawn's body lay, now covered with a white sheet.

"Well, let's do the scene, see what we have, and we'll talk about it later." I agreed and we approached the rest of the team where they stood talking and joking among themselves.

While some people might think we were uncaring or hard for standing around a murder scene joking, we knew it was the little jokes and small talk that helped us stay sane in moments like this. You could not take it personally, you could not show emotion, you had to do a job and put on a face that showed nothing. You had to pretend that the inhuman things that were done to people were normal, and not let anyone know that it tore at your heart and soul. If you laughed, people thought you were rude and disrespectful. If you cried, you were too attached and weak. If you got angry, people thought you were too tough and violent. You couldn't win, no matter what you did.

The scene investigation went quickly after we divided up the jobs. Jim started on the photography right away to get overalls of the scene before it was even more compromised than it already was. Then two guys went in to start searching and marking evidence. I partnered up with Matt Grover, a cop from a neighboring jurisdiction, to start the scene sketch.

Within a little over two hours, we had the scene completed. The logs were done and signed. The little bit of evidence that had been recovered had been photographed and collected, the preliminary sketch was completed, and the body was placed in a black body bag and removed by the coroner. Even he had no idea what might have caused the damage to Dawn's neck.

When everything was finished, we all packed up our gear and pulled the tape down from where it had been placed around the scene. I thanked everyone for coming out to help, told Jim I would talk to him in the afternoon when I came back in, and climbed into my truck.

I flipped up the cover to my mobile laptop, put my finger on the screen, and pushed the button for the forms. I chose the button that would display the Clear Incident form and typed "RTF" in the first field, which meant report to follow. On the second line, I typed, "Twenty-year-old female with throat ripped out." What else could I say—that was it. I hit the Send button and my computer beeped to tell me it had gone through.

It was time to head back to the station, warm up some of the old coffee that we had never gotten a chance to drink and start the paperwork.

CHAPTER EIGHT

JULIAN

he trip from New York to Fawn Hollow was uneventful. Gabriel was thrilled to ride in my midnight-blue 1968 Mustang. He had brought along a case of CDs and played a Trace Atkins song as soon as we were on the road. I had had this car for years, and there had been only one update made to it since I first acquired it: an updated stereo and five-disc CD player.

I allowed Gabe to play his music and we drove through the evening while he belted out the songs word for word. He had a great voice, and I didn't mind listening to the music. It was actually nice to have company for once, since I normally preferred to spend my time alone. He didn't ask questions, and there was little talk between us, just a comfortable quiet and the words of Trace singing songs about baseball and such.

When we turned up the driveway to the VMF-owned house, it was like walking back in time. Everything looked the same as the last time I had been there. It was the night I brought Calista here and we mated. I was not going to think about that right now—I couldn't afford to be sidetracked by the memories.

I drove over a bridge that crossed a gentle rolling creek and headed up a steep driveway that wound back into the woods. The house couldn't be seen from the roadway, it was too far back. As we pulled in front of the house, Gabe let out a whistle.

"Wow, this is incredible," he said with awe in his voice.

The house looked almost like a castle in the moonlight. Built in heavy stone, it was a large three-story house with massive windows around the bottom floor and smaller windows on the second floor with electric candles glowing in them. The caretakers knew we were coming and had lit the candles to welcome us. The third floor was where the sleeping chambers were and, from outside, people would think it was just attic space.

Gabe jumped out of the Mustang and hightailed it to the house to start his exploration, pushing open the door and walking in just as I climbed out of the car. I could hear him laughing from inside the house, and I smiled. He really was like a big kid. I stepped into the foyer to find that even after forty years, nothing appeared to have changed.

While the outside looked like a formidable castle, the inside looked like a beautiful country home. The smell of cinnamon spice and orange pledge came to my nose and I closed my eyes to inhale it. Cinnamon. When Calista and I had been together, it was as though our two scents mixed together perfectly to create the aroma of cinnamon and soft sugary dough just out of the oven.

I shook my head to clear the image and told Gabe to get a quick look around.

"You'll get a chance to explore later. We need to get over to the Taylors' residence and find out what's going on."

Alex sent me a text message just as we were leaving, saying we should head over there as soon as possible. His message gave just enough information for me to know that at least one of the females in the home had been a victim.

"Sure," Gabe called from down the hallway someplace. He was probably in the kitchen, digging through the fridge to see what was stocked inside.

He came back into view quickly saying, "Hey, did you know there was a hidden compartment in the fridge that has bags of blood in it?"

"Not very hidden if you found it in under three seconds," I said, and laughed. "Nice to know they stocked it up for us. Let's go." I turned to head out the door, not ready to spend any more time in this house quite yet. The memories were already weighing on my shoulders.

I heard Gabe whistle low as he stepped off the front landing. "Wow, look at the sky, it looks like a sea of stars." I didn't look up. I already knew what I would see, and the thought was like a stake through my soul.

CHAPTER NINE

KRISTIN

Okay, enough paperwork for now. I couldn't put it off any longer, and my brain was tired from trying to process all the information from the scene last night. I needed a break and I had to go back and talk to the Taylors again. *Might as well kill two birds with one stone*, I thought as I walked out of the station. I paused to look up at the night sky, releasing a dreamy sigh. Tonight, the stars stood out like sparkling diamonds in a sea of dark sapphires.

I called Mick on my cellphone after I was back in the truck. "Hey, I'm heading over to the Taylors'. I need to ask them some questions and let them know what's going on in the investigation."

"Okay," was all he answered before I said goodbye and hung up. He must be talking to someone if that was all the response I got.

As I drove, I thought about the message Detective Davis left me earlier. He said he was doing some research about the other cases he'd heard about, and that he would call me later. *Good*, I thought. We needed more information because we hadn't gotten much from the scene last night.

When I turned down Valley Spring Road, I was thinking about how the street curved sharply around the shale wall on the side. The road ran parallel to the Valley Spring Creek and there were no lights in this area, which made it extremely dark. As I went around a bend, I saw a dark-colored vehicle pulling out from a driveway in front of me. It was hard to see, and several things clicked into place.

First, the car was an older Mustang and it had no headlights on. Second, it was coming out of a driveway from a house that was unoccupied. Had they been at the house breaking in? I got behind the vehicle and could see there were two people in the car. Was it a guy and a girl coming back to the road after a private moment in the dark?

Don't know, but gonna find out. I flipped on my reds and blues and the vehicle's brake lights came on and then went off.

"Hey—don't you go taking off on me there, buddy," I said to myself, radio mic already in my hand as I prepared to call out my traffic stop. Our in-car computers didn't work very well in this area, so it was best to call out our stops directly on the radio.

The car in front of me started to slow down and eventually stopped after I hit my siren once to tell him that, yes, I was behind him, and I wanted him to stop—now.

Once the car did stop, I pulled up behind it, keeping about thirty feet between us. Without taking my eyes off the vehicle, I called out on the radio, "Thirty-One-Paul-One, traffic." I waited for my dispatcher to acknowledge before I continued.

"Thirty-One-Paul-One, proceed with your traffic," the voice radiated through the speaker behind my right shoulder.

"Thirty-One-Paul-One, I'll have a dark-colored older model Mustang stopped in the four hundred block of Valley Spring Road, New York registration N-I-T-E-1-3 occupied times two." Wait... Nite13...I was staring at the license plate. Okay, that is kind of ironic.

"Thirty-One-Paul-One, copy on the four hundred block of Valley Spring and the New York plate NITE13," the dispatcher repeated so I knew she understood where I was and with what.

The vehicle still hadn't turned on its headlights and there was little movement coming from inside. The brake lights went off as the driver put the car in park. I climbed slowly out of my truck and pulled my flashlight from my duty belt with my left hand, keeping the beam off the car until I was closer. I walked toward the vehicle, pausing for only a moment so that I could place my right hand on the back of the Mustang.

There were two reasons I did that. First, I wanted to make sure it was secure, and no one would jump out while I had my back to it; second, I wanted to place my fingerprints on the car. Should something happen to me, and they needed to search for the car, they could confirm it was the correct vehicle when they dusted the area and found my prints. It was something that we'd been trained to do, and it was habit now.

As I approached, I shined my flashlight into the driver's section of the car. The male driver sat with both hands on the wheel, facing forward. I could see he wore jeans and a leather jacket. *Kind of warm to be wearing a leather jacket*, I thought. My cop instinct kicked in. *What's he hiding?*

I stood slightly behind the driver's door and bent to get a quick look at the passenger. He was also staring straight ahead with his hands in his lap, a smile on his face. He was also wearing a leather jacket. My instincts heightened further, and my entire body tingled. I shifted back so that I was standing behind the driver's door more, resting my right hand on top of my firearm, ready to pull it if needed.

"Evening, sir. I'm Officer Greene from the Fawn Hollow Police Department. Are you aware that you were driving with your headlights off?" I asked in my most professional voice.

He stiffened as I spoke, and his mouth dropped open slightly. He gripped the steering wheel hard and began to turn in my direction, having to look over his shoulder to see me.

The moment our eyes met several things happened. First, I forgot I was a professional and completely put it out of my mind that I was on a traffic stop with an unknown vehicle. Then, I felt as if someone shot me with my own taser. My entire body stiffened and an electrical current slammed into me, although it wasn't painful. With our gazes locked, I felt as if we were having a conversation without words. My flashlight illuminated his face, and I was sucked in by the color of his eyes.

I stumbled back slightly. "Jewels, your eyes are like jewels."

His eyes grew wider, and he started to reach for the door handle. I may have been enthralled with his eyes, but instinct still had me moving. I gripped my Glock tightly while I waited to see what he was going to do.

I heard the other male in the car laugh and say, "Damn, Julian, you forgot to turn the headlights on." The passenger kept laughing.

The driver and I continued to stare at one another, silently observing and speaking volumes without saying a word. Holy shit, what was I supposed to be doing? Where was I? I couldn't think, couldn't speak. All I could do was stare at him. Something in the back of my mind tickled. I knew him...How did I know him? Cinnamon, did I smell cinnamon?

Suddenly, I realized that the lapel mic attached to my shirt was talking to me. I broke eye contact and instead stared at his neck, the skin over his vein pulsed wildly. "Thirty-One-Paul-One, status," a very loud, strong female voice said, filling the charged air.

Shit, I must have missed her calling me; she sounded worried. "Thirty-One-Paul-One, status okay," I replied quickly.

"Thirty-One-Paul-One, okay," she responded, her voice calmer now.

"I'm sorry, Officer," he said, and his voice caused a shiver to ripple up my spine. I met his gaze again. "We just pulled out of our driveway and I forgot to flip them on."

How do I know this man?

"You live there? I didn't think anyone lived there," I said quickly.

"It's actually owned by our company and we are staying there on business," he answered slowly. He had put both hands back on the wheel and I released the grip on my Glock but kept the heel of my hand rested on it.

His voice was like butter—soft, smooth—and for some odd reason, the scent of cinnamon wafted off of him. I could have listened to him talk all night. Inside, a voice said that I had listened to his voice deep into the night before. It reminded me of my dreams.

"Business? What kind of business?" I tried to keep him talking while I got a hold of myself long enough to do my job.

"Security Company, VMF Securities. We have a client in the area." He was studying me with wide eyes and speaking in a quiet tone.

I blinked, VMF? Wait, the Taylors were his clients? Why would the Taylors need a security company to help them with the death of their daughter? Did they think the police department couldn't do its job?

"You're here for the Taylors, aren't you?" I asked as I cocked my head to the side, scrutinizing him. His face was strong, handsome. His short brown hair was cut neatly around his head, showing off strong cheekbones and a prominent chin. His lips were full, and as I took them in, they parted, and I heard his sharp intake of breath. I felt my body begin to overheat.

Son of a bitch...my pulse was racing. Why the thought of reaching into the car and pulling him out through the window so I could wrap my arms around him and kiss those lips crossed my mind, I don't know. That was not normal for me. I tried to clear my mind, dislodge the image; it didn't work.

He glanced at my mouth, as I tried to control my breathing. I licked my dry lips and saw the look that crossed over his face. Damn, could he be thinking the same thing I was? Could he be feeling this current running between us? Was he wondering what it would feel like to come together and devour one another?

"Yes,"

I startled. "Yes, what?"

"Yes, we're here to see the Taylors. How did you know that?" He contemplated me with a thoughtful expression on his face.

"I'm the one who notified them. I heard them mention they needed to call the VMF," I replied.

He nodded once.

"I was just heading over to their house. I could show you where it is if you want to follow me." *Oh, please...please say yes. I want the chance to look into those eyes again.*

The passenger in the car leaned over, and I got a look at his handsome young face as he grinned. "Hey, that's ironic. Yeah, we'll follow you." He grinned up at me and I felt my body ease instantly.

"Okay, so follow me. It's not too much further, but the roads can be kind of tricky up ahead." I started to walk backward to my truck, my eyes staying on the driver.

He twisted in his seat as far as he could to watch me walk away. My hands were sweating, moisture ran down my back under my vest, and my heart continued to race. I swear there was some strange current zinging back and forth between us, and I would bet a thousand dollars that I knew that man from someplace.

Shit, I never even got his driver's license. I scrolled through the screens on my laptop that told me about the car. 1968 Mustang Coupe registered to a Julian Hutchinson of Poughkeepsie, New York. *Okay, so I know his name,* I thought as I hit the Clear button, adding no comments. I put the truck in drive to move around them and led them to the Taylors'.

As I looked in the rearview mirror, I saw the headlights snap on and the car began to follow me. It was only three miles to the Taylors' house, and already I was excited about looking into his eyes again.

CHAPTER TEN

JULIAN

I just pulled out of the driveway when I saw a flash of headlights coming around the corner behind us. The vehicle approached quickly, and within a few seconds, the bright red and blue lights of a police car flashed in the rearview mirror.

"Well, hell." I tapped the brakes when I first saw the lights, and thought maybe they needed to get around me—no reason they would be stopping me—but when the piercing tone of the siren went off once, I figured the cop wanted me to stop. I pulled over slowly and stopped.

"Hey, I've never been pulled over by the locals before," said Gabe, chuckling in the passenger's seat. "What did you do?"

"No idea. Just keep quiet. I'll deal with this." I sat facing forward with my hands on the steering wheel. I heard the door of the vehicle open behind me, and with the height of the lights hitting the inside of the car, I knew it had to be some kind of large truck that had stopped us.

As the officer cautiously approached my vehicle, I watched her walk up to the left side of the car by way of the side mirror. For some reason, she pushed down on the back of the car before moving forward and standing a few inches behind my window. The officer brought the flashlight up to the inside of the car and that is when her scent struck me like a brick upside the head. Sweet sugar and warmth flooded my nostrils and my mind started to reel. When the officer spoke, I felt as if the seat under me gave way and I was falling.

"Evening, sir. I'm Officer Greene from the Fawn Hollow Police Department. Are you aware that you were driving with your headlights off?" Her voice, oh my God, her voice. I had to relax my hand before I broke the steering wheel. It took every ounce of strength to turn my head and look at her, afraid that if I did, she wouldn't really be there.

The bright LED beam of her flashlight hit me square in the face and it took a second for my eyes to grow accustomed to the brightness. Our eyes met and it was as if time stood still. I was looking back at a memory. I knew my mouth was hanging open and I could do nothing but stare. She took a step back and I wanted to jump out of the car, pull her into my arms, and never let her go again.

"Jewels, your eyes are like jewels," she said. Holy fuck, my heart thundered in my chest—how could this be? How could she be here?

I couldn't think straight; I reached for the door handle and heard Gabe say in a low voice, "Don't even think about it."

She had seen the movement and stepped further away while flipping the strap that secured her firearm. Her hand wrapped around the handle tightly, ready to pull it out if needed.

Gabe said loudly enough for the officer to hear, "Damn, Julian, you forgot to turn the headlights on." He was laughing, but I heard the nervousness in it.

She shook her head slightly and reached for the mic that was attached by a clip to the front of her uniform shirt. "Thirty-One-Paul-One, status okay," she said. While she wasn't looking into my face, she still kept a wary eye on me.

When she asked if I lived in the house, I was surprised that she knew so much about the property and that no one was normally there. I was getting the impression she was damn good at her job. So much for the small police force that wouldn't know they were around. Shit.

A cop, she was a freaking cop!

I managed to keep my voice soft and slow even though my heart was still galloping wildly within my chest. The more she spoke, the more I wanted to jump out of the car and pull her to me.

I saw something flash across her face when I mentioned our company name. Did she somehow recognize it?

"You're here for the Taylors, aren't you?" She was studying me now. I watched her lick her lips as her eyes passed over my mouth. I almost lost my mind right then. White heat flashed through my body. I sucked in a shaky breath and remembered she had asked me a question.

I was trying to search the features of her face but finding it hard with the bright light directly in my face. I could see the outline of her features but not the details. I needed to see the details. I needed to look into her eyes.

There was raw pain in her voice when she mentioned notifying the Taylors, but it turned professional again while she stated she was actually on her way over there herself. Talk about irony, or fate, or whatever. Who the fuck cared! She was standing right here in front of me. How?

When she said we could follow her, I almost told her I would follow her to the gates of hell if she'd let me. Gabe took that moment to jump into the conversation and before I knew it, she was slowly walking backward to her truck, watching me as I turned to take in every detail I could of her. Even though I knew I would be right behind her and see her again soon, I didn't want to tear my eyes off her for a second.

"Holy shit, man." Gabe said from the seat next to me. "You okay? I've never seen you act that way. You, like, froze and I could feel your pulse and all these crazy emotions coming off you. What the hell was that all about?"

"I'll explain later." But how could I explain it to him when I didn't understand it myself? I put the car in drive and remembered to turn on the headlights when the white police Expedition pulled in front of us.

In just three minutes, my entire life had been flipped upside down. Questions were swirling in my mind. The possibilities of what those answers could be whirled around in the mix. I followed the truck and wished that I were sitting inside it with her. When we pulled up in front of a two-story Colonial house, I felt as if I was going to snap with the tension that had built inside of me.

I parked in the driveway next to her truck and glanced at Gabe, who was staring at me. "What?"

"Dude, I have never seen you this amped up before—you all right? It's like that cop crawled under your skin the moment her mouth opened." He studied me hard waiting for an answer, but I only shook my head and climbed out of the car. I didn't know how to even respond to him, but he was right. She was under my skin, in my head, and running straight through my veins.

She had already started walking up to the door. She had wide shoulders for a woman, and her waist looked thin, but with her gun belt on, it was hard to really tell. We followed up the path behind her toward the front door.

As she reached the door, it swung open and I heard a man's voice coming from inside of the house. "Kristin, I'm surprised to see you. I thought you were someone else."

Kristin, her name was Officer Kristin Greene.

"Mr. Taylor, I'm sorry. I should have called to tell you I was stopping by, but I'm not alone—I think I found the people you were waiting for." She didn't turn around, but kind of tipped her head our way as if pointing. The man stepped forward and looked in our direction as we came closer.

"Ah, yes. Mr. Hutchinson and Mr. Montgomery, I presume. Won't you all please come in?" He stepped back and, with a wave of his hand, allowed us to pass by. He looked me in the eye and nodded, and then looked at the officer with narrowed eyes before glancing at me again. I understood: *Play it quiet in her presence.*

"Mr. Taylor, I'm Julian Hutchinson and this is Gabriel Montgomery." I offered my hand, even though it was not a normal thing for vampire men to do. He took it and seemed to understand why I offered it. Kristin had turned around and while she wasn't looking at us, she was looking in our direction, watching intently.

"Hey, Mr. Taylor, you can call me Gabe," he said from behind me as I stepped further into the house. He offered his hand right away and looked around. "Great house you got here!" he said while looking around the foyer and up to the landing on the second floor.

Right then a woman stepped out of a door upstairs and looked down: Gina Marie Taylor. I had not known that she was the mother of the girl who was killed. She was taller and more attractive than she had been when I first met her. She seemed alarmed that Kristin stood in the entry with us, flipping her gaze back and forth between the two of us. Her mind seemed to come to a quick decision about something and she nodded at me.

Jesus, she knew. I gasped when I realized this—I wasn't losing my mind. How long had she known?

"Julian, what a pleasure it is to see you again. It has been a long time," she said softly as she started down the stairs. "I didn't realize you were still working for VMF."

"Gina Marie, hello. Yes, it has been a while." I eyed her hard and wanted to ask her why she hadn't found me and told me. I tried to send her a message, but her walls were up. I managed to keep my voice level, even though it was on the verge of shaking.

"Kristin, what a pleasure it is to see you again. We didn't expect to see you tonight. Since you are here, please, won't you join us?" She put her hand on Kristin's arm as she finished the sentence.

"Mrs. Taylor, um…I'm sorry to interrupt with your company." She kept her eyes on Mrs. Taylor; she hadn't looked me in the face since we arrived.

I wanted her to look at me. *Look at me, look at me—I need to see your eyes,* my mind screamed. I think I took a step back when I heard a reply.

No, I can't look.

Everyone except Kristin turned to me; it must have been the small gasp I'd made when I heard her voice inside my head.

Gina Marie looked away nervously. She pulled Kristin into the living room. Kristin continued as if nothing had happened. "I have a few questions to ask you and Mr. Taylor, and then I will be on my way. I don't want to be in the way of your guests." She spoke in a polite, professional voice. A voice I had longed for years to hear again.

"Sure, of course. Why don't we sit down?" Gina Marie moved her hand from Kristin's arm to her elbow and guided her to a seat. Mr. Taylor motioned for us to follow.

Once inside, Mr. and Mrs. Taylor got comfortable on a loveseat and Kristin sat on the edge of the sofa near them, while Gabe plopped himself down in a wingback chair, looking way too big for it. I walked over near the windows and pretended to look out but was instead trying to gain some sort of composure. My mind was in a whirlwind and I couldn't get my heart to stop thumping wildly. *What if?* I kept thinking...*What if?*

CHAPTER ELEVEN

KRISTIN

*O*kay, so that was weird. I felt Julian staring at me, and it was almost as if he was willing me to look at him, until I told myself, *No, I can't look*. Then the room fell into complete and utter silence. Had I spoken out loud? I didn't think so. Everyone's gaze shifted between the two of us.

When we had first arrived at the Taylors', I realized that I had better keep myself in check, and the best way to do that was not to look at him—at all! I didn't know what came over me out there on the street, but I needed to do my interview and get the hell out of here as fast as possible. Whatever passed between us out in the dark was nothing I could deal with right now.

I watched the Taylors sit down on a blue and white striped love seat, and I sat on the edge of the matching couch as close to them as I could get. The tall, blond, young man who referred to himself as Gabe made his way over to one of the side chairs and dropped down into it as if he had lived there his whole life. I chuckled silently. He seemed like a kid stuck in a man's body.

I didn't look at Julian, but I knew he had walked over to the windows, his back to the room. I didn't have to look at him to feel him. Somehow, I could feel the hum of his energy in the room all around me. The scent of cinnamon swirled around the room, along with the sweet smell of plums, fresh breezes, and pine trees.

I turned my attention back to the Taylors and prepared myself for what I needed to do. This conversation would've been easier if these other two men were not here, but I was professional enough to move forward. For a moment, I wondered how they could be so composed. How could you lose a daughter and then seem happy when guests showed up at your door? It didn't make sense, but none of this was making sense.

"I need to speak to you about your daughter," I paused and glanced toward Julian and Gabriel.

Mr. Taylor responded, "Whatever you want to ask, you can do so in front of them."

I nodded abruptly. "Mrs. Taylor, how are you doing today, are you holding up okay?" I asked sincerely. I could not imagine what it would feel like to lose a child, and yet she didn't appear to be in mourning at all until I spoke.

She smiled sweetly. "I'm doing as well as I can be. It's hard to believe." She had tears in her eyes, but they did not fall. Okay, this was still so strange. If I had lost a child, I would think I'd be a blubbering mess. I watched her intently, trying to figure her out. "I know that I will see her again someday, so I'm okay." She gave me a small smile.

"I need to ask you both a few questions about last night. I hope you understand. I do realize this is a hard time for you, but it is something that needs to be done." I bounced my words between them as I spoke.

Mr. Taylor responded, "Of course, Kristin, we understand—and we will answer your questions as best as we can." He glanced at Julian's back as he spoke the last part. I took a peek in his direction and saw that Julian's back was rigid and his arms were crossed over his chest. It made his back look wider and stronger inside the leather jacket. Oh, to run my hands over that back...

Mrs. Taylor brought me back to reality when she cleared her throat. I peered at her, embarrassed to have been caught staring at him, and looked down at the floor to collect my thoughts again.

"When was the last time you saw Dawn?" I finally asked.

"I saw her yesterday afternoon before she left for work. She worked down at Kohl's. She was supposed to be home around nine thirty last night. When she didn't get home right away, we figured she must have gone out with friends." Mrs. Taylor was looking intently at me as she spoke. "So I called down to the store today to find out what time she left, and they said she never came to work. Wasn't even scheduled to work, so we don't know exactly where she went when she left here."

"Did you call any of her friends, ask if they were with her or had heard from her last night?"

"I did," she answered, appearing happy to have done something like this. "I called all her friends, but no one had spoken with her. Lori, her friend from work, said she had just started seeing a new guy. She didn't know his name, but said he was new to the area."

"Okay. I'll need Lori's phone number so I can follow up with her myself," I said.

"Of course, we'll get it for you," Mr. Taylor stated.

"Did you know she was seeing someone?" I asked, looking at Mr. Taylor, but thinking Mrs. Taylor would probably be the one to answer. I was correct.

"No, she didn't mention anyone." She seemed disappointed that she had not known there was a man in her daughter's life.

I took a deep breath and started in on some of the harder questions I had. I looked directly into Mr. Taylor's eyes and asked him, "Sir, last night when I came in, how did you know she was dead?"

Before he could stop himself, he replied, "I could smell her on you." He glanced at Gabe and Julian once the words left his mouth.

"Excuse me, sir, but how did you smell her on me?" Did he mean he could smell her perfume or something? I watched him carefully, but out of the corner of my eye, I could see Julian looking at Mr. Taylor, his eyebrow raised.

Mr. Taylor cleared his throat and struggled to come up with an answer for my question. I couldn't wait to hear this.

"I don't know, maybe it was her perfume. Maybe I didn't smell her on you at all. Maybe I was just worried about her having not come home and when you showed up so serious, I knew something must be wrong." He appeared to be giving me an honest answer, almost. I regarded him carefully as I continued.

"Mrs. Taylor, last night you mentioned that someone's back. Who's back? What did you mean by that?" I looked at her with critical eyes, wanting to know how much she was going to tell me that would be the truth. In my mind, I heard the words whispered in a deep, husky voice, *You're good*.

What the hell?

"Oh! You heard that, did you? Um, well…" Mrs. Taylor didn't quite have an answer for that and seemed to be trying to figure out what to say when Julian interrupted.

"Officer, this family has been under our protection for some time. There was a man who was stalking them several years ago. I believe the Taylors think it might be connected." As he talked, he walked toward the chair that Gabe sat in. He stood behind the chair and placed one hand on the top, looking deeply into my eyes.

Oh, dear God, in the light, his eyes were even more incredible than they had been outside under my flashlight. Here, I could see the dark color of sapphires around the outside of his eyes and the bright clear color of aquamarines around the center of his pupil. *Sapphires and aquamarines—oh my God, his eyes are beautiful.*

"Glad you think so," the strange voice chuckled in my mind again. My eyes narrowed and I shook my head. I swear I was hearing things.

I went back to checking him out and noticed his shoulders were almost as wide as the chair. His dark blue shirt clung tightly to his massive chest and I could see just a few brown hairs coming out of the top of his shirt near his neck.

A throat cleared in the room and I looked down at my boots trying to remember what he had just said. After another second, I turned to the Taylors and asked them, "What's this guy's name?"

They both looked at Julian. Why did they feel like they needed his permission to answer a question?

"Because they do," replied the husky masculine voice in my head.

Was this just because his company had offered them protection in the past? What was going on here? I knew something was up, but I just didn't get it.

"Officer—" he started, then stopped and waited until I gave him my attention before he continued. "Maybe it would be best if I could speak with the Taylors first, and then I could help you with the information that I have learned from them."

Wait a fucking second. Who the hell was this guy, and why did he think he could just march in here and take over my investigation? My eyes flared; I felt the anger starting to boil under my skin. *"It's not your investigation,"* a very cocky voice stated firmly in my mind. Jesus, I must be more tired than I thought, but anger was pulling at me now.

"Sir, this incident is under police investigation, it is not something that your security company can handle. If the Taylors are in danger, then it is our job to know these things so we can offer them protection and stop this person if he is the one who is responsible," I said hotly, and wasn't ready to stop yet. "Refusing to provide information to us during an investigation is an obstruction of justice, and I would think the Taylors would want this guy found."

I stared straight at him, and a flash of joy sparked in his eyes.

"Kristin—" he started to speak, but I interrupted him immediately.

"It's Officer Greene to you, Mr. Hutchinson," I said coolly.

He chuckled. "Okay, Officer Greene, I am sure that the Taylors would like nothing more than for your department to catch this guy, but we have worked with them for many years and we know information that might help with your investigation. So it seems like it would be a good idea if we could question them, and then we could sit down with you and go over the information afterward." He had a smirk on his face that I wanted to wipe off.

"Who the hell are you, a lawyer?" I managed to say without barking at him.

"No, I'm an enforcer," he said with a straight face and a very deep voice. "It's just like your position—I figure out what's going on, and then I enforce what needs to be done."

My eyes were hard, and I could only believe that right this second, they were probably steel-gray. *Enforcer, my ass! More like a freaking hit man!* When the word *"similar"* ran through my brain, I gaped at him like I had just been shocked. His eyes narrowed slightly, and the corner of his mouth turned as if he was about to smile.

I heard my dispatcher calling my partner, and while I kept my eyes on Julian, I bent my head down to listen closer to my radio mic. "Thirty-One-Paul-Four, you have a physical domestic at Twenty-Two Forty-Four Riverdale Drive." Shit, I had to go.

I glared at Julian another moment before turning to the Taylors. "I'm sorry, but I have to go and help my partner. Would you mind giving Mr. Hutchinson my phone number, and he can call me when he's done here? I'll meet up with him then and we can discuss this." I glanced at him pointedly, saying in my mind, *and you will tell me what the fuck is going on!*

A seductive smile spread over his lips as I heard the voice in my head again. *"Maybe, maybe not."*

Did he really just answer me?

Before I could do or say anything else, I picked up on a piece of information on my radio that told me I needed to move quickly. I made for the front door with a quick goodbye over my shoulder to the Taylors.

Running out to my truck, I was trying to figure out what all this was about. Had I really heard him talking in my head, or was I just reading his body language? I didn't allow myself to think anything more about it as I jumped into my vehicle and backed out of the driveway, flipping my lights on and grabbing my mobile radio mic.

"Thirty-One-Paul-One, put me en route to Paul-Four's domestic."

CHAPTER TWELVE

JULIAN

The shock was starting to dim, and I began to put things into perspective. When I first saw her, I didn't believe it could be real. When we arrived at the Taylors' house and she answered me through my mind, without even knowing she was doing it, it was as if someone punched me in the stomach.

I found myself listening in on her thoughts while she was asking questions. She was smart, but then I already knew that. She had no idea what was going on, although she knew there was more than met the eye. That was both good and bad. I still didn't know if it could be true, but in my heart and soul I begged it to be.

I was serious about wanting to speak with the Taylors first. The flash of her eyes—the spark of fight that ignited as they glowed green, then turned to a steel-gray—that was the final confirmation I needed. I found myself fighting back the urge to grin, to shout, "Thank you, God," into the room as she tried to hold her anger in check. It was glorious, amazing!

As she got up and started toward the door, I could smell frustration coming off her in waves and it was the most incredible scent I had smelled in years. I watched every movement as she ran down the path and got into her truck. As she pulled out of the driveway, she flipped on the lights and took off down the roadway.

"It's her, isn't it, Gina Marie?" I asked quietly, closing my eyes, afraid that I was making this all up.

"I believe it is, Julian," she said, just as softly.

"Who is she supposed to be?" Gabe asked.

We both ignored him, and I turned to face Gina Marie. Mr. Taylor was watching me. He didn't comment, though I assumed he knew what we were talking about.

"How long have you known?" I asked.

"Ten years ago, I saw her. The moment I spoke with her, I thought it had to be her. It was only when I saw the two of you together that I was absolutely positive. I know you are wondering why I didn't find you and tell you, but she was young, so far from being ready for our culture, and she was involved with a human. I wasn't sure if it was too late, and I didn't want to hurt you if it was." She smiled sadly. "How long did it take you to figure out?" she asked.

"Who is she supposed to be?" Gabe asked again, looking eager to be part of the conversation.

"Instantly…I knew it the moment her scent entered my nose. I knew it was Calista…"

CHAPTER THIRTEEN

KRISTIN

he domestic turned out to be a total mess, and Mick and I were stuck arresting both the male and female parties after he beat her up and she then stabbed him with a knife in the arm. Normally, that might be considered self-defense. At first, it was going to be the male who was arrested, but after we threw him to the ground and wrestled him into cuffs, the female turned on us.

It's actually more common than you would think. People got all hot and angry during domestics and called the police to come rescue them, but as soon as we got there and took someone into custody, the victim suddenly changed their story. "No, it was my fault, they didn't do anything wrong." Even when there was physical evidence, like a split lip or a swollen eye, the sight of someone in cuffs could flip a person quick.

The female threw a punch at me just as I got up off the ground, dragging her husband to his feet. It caught me off guard and pushed me back against the wall, since I was off balance when she did it. Her man was so excited by her turning against us that he started yelling at her, "Go, girl—you get 'em!" It had ended up with him face first into the ground again with Mick sitting on his back and her being tased by me. We then took them both out in handcuffs and shackles.

By the time we got them locked away down in the central booking station and I got back to the station, my jaw ached, and I had a headache. Plus, my stomach was growling from not eating all night. I grabbed a snack bar out of my file drawer where I kept a stash for just these types of nights and plopped down in an office chair to start the paperwork.

Mick was at his computer beside me munching on a sandwich and the two of us talked over charges and laughed about the incident while we worked. I had enough to think about to keep me busy and allowed only a little bit of my brain to mull over the incident at the Taylors' house tonight.

Julian—it wasn't just his eyes that were beautiful, it was his whole body. He wasn't a big man. Not much taller than me, maybe a couple of inches, but he just conveyed this raw kind of strength. He was an incredible piece of human flesh. I wanted to know what he felt like up close, what he tasted like on my tongue. Was the scent of cinnamon really coming from him, and what would his voice sound like whispered in my ear?

I kept trying to shove him to the back of my mind, but the niggling feeling that I had seen him before, that I knew him, kept bringing him right back to the front. It was as if I had all the pieces to a puzzle, but I just didn't know how to fit them together.

Finally, after struggling with the mental puzzle and pushing myself to get the reports done, I finished my criminal complaint and incident report and helped Mick with his. By the time it was all done, it was time for us to get ready for shift change; our night was over.

I walked out to my truck to grab my gear and had the strong feeling that I was being watched. I set my gear bag down slowly on the driveway and turned around to look out at the trees behind our station. I didn't see anything, so I let my hearing fan out to see if it could pick anything up. I stood with my eyes closed and reached with my hearing. I heard nothing, but as I reached down for my bag, I caught a light scent on the air, leather and cinnamon. A smile eased up my lips and I stood and faced directly toward the tree line.

"You're out there watching me, aren't you?" I thought.

A single word vibrated softly through my head, *"Yes,"* followed by a soft husky chuckle that traveled straight down to my groin.

Surprised by the sexual feeling that hit me, I laughed it off and returned to the station. "Kris, you're really losing it," I said to myself as I entered the locker room.

It had been so long since I'd been the least bit interested physically in a man, that seeing this handsome stranger tonight had conjured up all these little fantasies that he would be even a little bit interested in me. Who was I kidding?

When our relief showed up, we explained what we had dealt with overnight and headed out to the garage to pull our private vehicles out of the bays and shelter our patrol cars. I climbed into my Jeep and called out to Mick to enjoy his two days off.

We normally worked twelve-hour rotating schedules and we generally never worked more than two days in a row except for the weekend, which was three days. We had just finished up our weekend shifts, so we were off for two days. Although, I only had one day off because I had picked up a shift for someone else.

I almost wished I wasn't going to be off at all. I wanted to speak with Julian, but maybe it would be better if I didn't. After all, I couldn't go making a pass at him in the middle of a murder investigation. I laughed at the thought of making a pass at anyone and pulled out onto the road to drive home as the sky was breaking into a light shade of blue, announcing the coming of another day.

When I got home, Garda was eager and waiting by the garage door. I dropped my shoulder bag and let him outside to relieve himself. The poor guy was alone in the house for nine hours without being able to go out. It was a good thing that I found a great pet sitter who was willing to come over and let him out around nine o'clock at night so that he wouldn't have to hold his bladder for thirteen hours.

After he was finished and had a chance to chase a bunny around the yard, I fixed him his breakfast and went to shower and put on pajamas. Sleep was going to be a welcome thing today. I was feeling the effects of the busy weekend shift. After spending twelve hours in twenty pounds of gear, it was an awesome feeling to stand under the hot spray of the shower and then pull on my favorite cotton bottoms and T-shirt.

I let Garda out once more before I found myself dragging my feet to bed. I knew the pet sitter would come during the morning and take Garda out for a nice walk, so I didn't feel guilty for saying good night and walking down the hall to my bedroom.

Once I made sure that my bedroom shutters were closed tight and the shades were drawn to make my room look like it was actually midnight and not sunrise, I climbed under the cool sheets and pulled my quilt up under my chin.

Julian's face filled my mind the moment my lids were closed. What would it be like to stand in front of him and look into the depths of his jewel-colored eyes? How would he feel under my hands as I caressed them over his chest? How would his lips feel as they touched mine?

I quickly slipped off to sleep and joined in on one of my many long-standing dreams...

I was lying under the dark sky, staring up at the stars, the cold metal under me. I arched my back as my pants were slid down my legs and I felt large, strong male hands slide up the inside of my thigh. His fingers slipped into my wet heat, finding that one spot that would take me over the edge. I moaned and shook as I reached an orgasm almost immediately. It was then that I was pulled up into his arms and, for the first time in my dream, I saw the face of the man. Julian's face was in front of me. He pulled back his lips and I saw his fangs. I was neither surprised nor afraid as he put his mouth to my neck and bit me. It seemed only natural for me to bite him back...

When I awoke several hours later, the dream came back to me quickly. Damn...I needed to either make sure I ate before I went to bed or got laid soon. What a strange twist to the dream. Okay—not strange, as I'd had most of that dream before, but I had never seen a face to go with the body, and what possessed me to give him fangs? In previous dreams, I had felt him bite my neck, but not with the incredible burst of passion that this had been. Talk about making him a bad boy, geez. Other than those things, the dream was always the same. Always the dark sky with the stars, always outside on top of a car. Car

—wait—I sat up in bed, my eyes wide. The car in my dreams was a midnight-blue Mustang. Holy. Crap! That was the car Julian was driving. Okay, okay—wait. Maybe that was the reason I put his face in the dream, because he was the one driving the car.

That would normally make sense, but for the first time, the dream felt real, not like a dream at all. More like a memory. I glanced at the clock and found it was just after one. I had slept six hours, more than normal coming off a night shift.

I climbed out of bed, said hello to Garda, and let him outside to run around in the sunshine before I turned on the coffee pot. I might have gotten more sleep than I normally did, but I still needed my caffeine fix.

I sat down waiting for the coffee to brew and picked up my cell-phone to check my messages. I had two voicemails and several e-mails. I checked my voicemails first while waiting for my coffee to be ready. My eyes weren't open enough to read the e-mails yet. The first message was from Jim Davis. He had some information about the incidents that had happened over in the next county that were similar to ours. He told me to call him when I got up.

The second voicemail made me stop breathing. "Hello, Kristin—I mean, Officer Greene. It's Julian Hutchinson. We met last night. I wasn't sure if I should call or send you an e-mail, so I did both. I'd like to set up a time to meet with you to talk about what's going on. I won't be available until early evening, so it might be best if you send me an e-mail with a time and a place that we can meet for dinner. Hope you slept well today. I'll talk with you soon, Kristin."

Oh my God! How could I possibly be turned on from just hearing his voice? And the way he said my name—it made me want to melt. I listened to the message two more times, not really listening to the words, hearing only the strength and heat in his voice.

I poured my coffee, let Garda back in, and climbed into my glider with my phone in my lap. I was anxious to see what the e-mail said, but I was trying to control my excitement. What was up with this? It was hard to believe I was a grown woman, the way I was acting.

With Garda lying at my feet, I found my way to my e-mail. I first looked at my work e-mail but didn't find anything from anyone's address that I didn't recognize. Maybe it got caught in the spam folder. I would have to sign on from my computer to see it if that was the case.

That was okay, I was kind of glad it wasn't there. It gave me more time to wonder what he had written. I took a sip of my coffee. Thank God, Dunkin Donuts started selling its beans. There was nothing like a fresh cup of Dunkin Donuts coffee in the morning—okay afternoon. I took a deep whiff of it as I took another sip and then set it back down.

I went back to my phone to check my other e-mail accounts, figuring they were full of friends checking on me or sending me silly forwards that I never took the time to read. As I opened one of my accounts, I saw an e-mail from a JHutchinson. How the hell did he get my private e-mail account?

I opened the e-mail and found my fingers were shaking as I started to read it.

Kristin...Gina Marie passed along this e-mail address to me. I find it ironic that if you take my license plate "Nite13" and your license plate "Wolf69" you come up with Nitewolf1369...your e-mail address. Isn't that kinda crazy?

Okay...that was strange, but what was even stranger was how the hell he knew what my license plate was. The thought occurred to me that maybe he really had been watching me last night when I'd gotten ready to leave work.

I want to see you tonight; I know you are off. We have a lot to talk about. A lot to catch up on. I will be available after seven tonight. Name a place and I will meet you there for dinner. Until then. Jules

He wanted to see me? That thought made me excited and flustered at the same time. What could we possibly have to catch up on? Was he just talking about the case? The way he wrote it sounded like we were long-lost friends and we should be going out for a beer to catch up on old times.

How did he know I wasn't working tonight? Or that I would want to see him on my night off? I was torn between being excited and being pissed off. I was tempted to either ignore his e-mail or write back and say I was busy tonight.

Instead, after starting and stopping an e-mail to him over and over, I simply wrote:

Riverwood Café – 7:30

I hit the Send button before I could second-guess myself. A tingle of something ran up my spine—fear, anticipation, excitement, lust? Who knew, maybe a little of all of them combined.

I closed my e-mail and decided to take Garda for a run. I needed some way to let off this pent-up energy and running would do just that.

I decided I'd call Detective Davis on my way to the park, that way, I could think about things while I ran. I went to my room to throw on some running clothes, all the while considering with a little excitement about what I should wear tonight.

CHAPTER FOURTEEN

JULIAN

*A*fter Calista, I mean Kristin, left the Taylors', we went over all the details we knew about the night before. They had heard that Damon might be back in the area but hadn't been worried that he would find them. They had been very careful to keep quiet about what they were, never socializing with their own kind. Of all people, Gina Marie knew what Damon was capable of.

When we were done talking, it was decided that Gabriel would stay at the house with the Taylors in case Damon came after Gina Marie. They would pretend he was a cousin from down south if anyone asked.

Gina Marie gave me Kristin's personal phone number and e-mail address. When I saw the e-mail address, I looked up at her.

"I know," she said. "Kind of ironic, don't ya think?" She laughed.

When I left the house, I wasn't ready to head back to the VMF house quite yet. I was way too keyed up, so I found my way over to the police station and found a place to park my car so I could walk on foot and stand in the tree line behind the building.

The old white ranch house was an odd choice for a police station. If it wasn't for the large garage to the side of the building where the patrol cars were kept, and the brightly lit sign out front, you could've easily passed right by it without noticing it.

I wasn't there long before Kristin and another cop walked out the side door. They were laughing about something as they went to their cars. Kristin walked over to the passenger side of the truck and pulled out a large black bag. As she did so, she stopped and focused back toward the trees.

Oh, her instincts were good, damn good. She knew someone was watching her. I bet that helped her out a lot with her job. I stopped moving and breathing while she searched the trees. I was back far enough that no matter how good her eyes were, she wouldn't be able to see me without being a full-blooded vampire. I knew that as a half-breed, her eyesight was probably better than most, but not quite at its peak, yet.

I noticed that she lifted her nose up into the air. Wow...now she smelled the breeze for what she knew was out there, but couldn't see. I saw the smile on her lips as I heard the words cross my mind, *"You're out there watching me, aren't you?"*

"Yes," I answered back.

I almost laughed out loud when she looked shocked at my response. She didn't really believe that it was me. She thought she was making things up. Little did she know how I really felt about her. I listened to her mental chatter for a little while longer, shaking my head, while she wondered why someone like me would be interested in her. God, if she only knew.

When she pulled her Jeep out of the garage and I saw the back of the SUV, I could not believe it said "Wolf69." Between my license plate and her license plate, it made up the e-mail address Gina Marie had given to me. Somehow, she remembered. How was that possible?

When she pulled out of the driveway, looking tired, I jogged back to my car, peering up at the lightening sky. I would have just enough time to get back to the VMF house before the sun rose.

We could tolerate a small amount of sun. Only the very old of our kind would burst into flames by a ray of sunlight. The longer we existed, the more the sun affected us. As I was just over a hundred, I could tolerate the soft rays of the sunrise or sunset, but not for very long before I grew uncomfortable.

When I arrived back at the house, it felt different this time. I wasn't dreading it. In fact, I actually looked forward to seeing the inside now. I wanted to remember the times that I had shared with her. For a moment, I was nervous. Would she fall in love with me again? What if she didn't? What if she was so different now that she didn't see me as the man that she had known so many years ago? What if I had changed too much since then?

I'll cross that bridge if I come to it. No matter what I do, I will not lose her again. I can't.

I walked into the house carrying my one duffel bag and made my way into the kitchen. It had been a long time since I had last fed, and I pulled a large bag of blood out of the hidden compartment. I warmed it in the microwave after pouring it into a mug. It was so much better when it was warm, not anywhere near as incredible as right-from-the-source blood, nothing matched that. My mind flipped back to the moment I had bit into Calista's neck the first time. Would I find that same satisfaction when I bit into Kristin's neck now?

After the microwave beeped, I grabbed the mug and my duffel bag and headed upstairs to the room we had once made love in.

At the top of the third floor, I walked down the hall to the second door on the right. It was already open, and a light was shining on the nightstand. There were no windows, and the only difference to the room now was the bedspread that lay across the king-sized bed.

I dropped my bag onto the floor and sat on the edge of the bed, kicking off my boots before pushing myself back against the pillows. As I took a deep drink from my mug, my fangs elongated. The smell of blood normally started that process immediately, but my mind was so engrossed in other thoughts that it wasn't until the blood hit my tongue that my fangs extended.

I laid my head down and recalled that night so long ago in this very room.

When we had finished our initial lovemaking outside under the stars, I carried Calista up to the bedroom. We climbed in the shower, taking the time to kiss each other and touch every inch that we could. Afterward, we lay in bed for hours talking, laughing, and making love over and over.

Neither one of us thought about what time it was until it was too late. A knock on the bedroom door preceded the door opening with Alex on the other side. Shock was evident in his eyes as he took in the two of us wrapped around one another in the bed. Alex had been angry. There was no doubt about it. He stood in the doorway glaring at the two of us for a long time before I finally spoke.

"Alex, I'm sorry," I said as I tried to sit up.

"Don't, Julian...don't you dare," he snapped before he turned and walked out, slamming the door behind him.

We stayed quiet, listening to the house until we heard the front door bang shut. He must have slammed it really hard for us to have heard it up on the third floor. I remember looking back at Calista. She spoke softly. "I know I should feel bad about doing this to him. But right now, I am having a hard time feeling bad about it when you are making me feel so good about this." She pulled me back down and kissed me long and hard.

We never looked back after that, and Alex never forgave us for what happened. Although he had eventually accepted it, especially when he heard that we had a child on the way, none of us ever spoke about it.

Man, wait until he hears about this! What was he going to do?

I sat back up on the edge of the bed and figured enough time had passed now that I could probably call Kristin and leave her a message. I was hoping she turned off her phone while she slept, and I wouldn't have to speak with her just yet. The next time I spoke with her, I wanted it to be face to face, just the two of us.

I pulled the piece of paper out of my pocket with her phone number and e-mail address on it. I still couldn't believe her e-mail address, as if somewhere in her soul she remembered.

I dialed the phone and was glad when it went straight to voicemail. I didn't think I would be able to handle hearing her sleepy voice right now. After sending the e-mail, I pulled off my clothes and lay back in the bed nude. The intimate memories of our time together gave me a hard-on and I fisted my dick, stroking it slowly, imagining Kristin doing it. I pictured making love to her, visualizing our past, predicting our future, and had no trouble relieving myself quickly. After cleaning up, I drifted off into a delicate sleep filled with memories of our life together and dreams of our future. I would not dream of the night she was taken from me or think about it ever happening again.

I had found her, and I would never lose her again. I made that vow as I drifted off to sleep.

CHAPTER FIFTEEN

KRISTIN

*M*y run was productive today. Garda and I pushed ourselves and managed to finish a solid five-mile steady run. When I was done, I wasn't sure who was more tired. I think Garda might have been ready to quit at four miles, but I pushed him.

Those five miles gave me a lot of time to think over what Detective Davis told me when we spoke earlier. He'd gone to meet with detectives in the next county who had been working two similar cases. Both of them were double homicides, and both were mother and daughter pairs.

It reminded me of when Mrs. Taylor said something about being next. Was she? Was she supposed to have died like the others? After hearing about the other homicides, instinct told me that there was something to be concerned about. Especially since the manner in which it was done was almost exactly the same as the homicide that we had. The only difference was that all four of the other bodies had holes in their chests, and Dawn's had not.

What I wanted to know was how the Taylors knew about all of this and why it would be important for them to know if she had been stabbed in the chest. From what Detective Davis said, very little information was given out about the other homicides, and the fact that there had been holes in their chests was not released to the press—and no one had even asked this question, as far as we knew.

Also, what was the connection between the two sets of those killed and the family I was now dealing with? There had to be a connection. With what was done, and in the manner that it occurred, it looked to be a true hate crime.

Both of the women had been in their mid-thirties and the two children had been eight and fifteen. Both were soccer mom types who didn't fall into the category of sneaking behind their husbands' backs to have affairs, and definitely didn't seem the drug type, although both of those ideas were totally possible in today's world. I mean we were seeing more and more soccer moms enjoying a hit off something to get through the day.

It seemed as if the more questions we got answered, the more answers we needed. Hopefully, the meeting tonight with Julian would give me some of them.

Julian. The thought of seeing him again had been on the edge of my mind during the whole run. I wasn't sure if I was more excited or nervous to see him. I kept telling myself that this was business and I shouldn't feel either way about it. There had been many times I met up with other cops or detectives for a quick bite or a beer to discuss a case. So why did this feel different?

And why did I have to pick the Riverwood Café, of all places? That was the place where Trevor and I used to go on a regular basis to unwind and relax. I thought repeatedly to send Julian another e-mail and change the location. Maybe switch it to the sports bar at the other end of the plaza, where it would be loud and bright, instead of the quiet romantic setting of the café.

"Does it really matter?" I asked out loud and threw in a load of laundry. When I had gotten home from my run, I decided to get some work done around the house—a quick vacuum, some laundry, and a load of dishes passed the rest of the day until it was time for me to jump in the shower and get ready for my meeting with Julian. Maybe subconsciously I was tidying up the house in case I brought him back here, not that I would. Okay, maybe. Ugh! No. No! I would not!

I looked in my closet and again wondered what I should wear. I was never a picky dresser. Normally, when I went out with friends, I threw on jeans and a blouse. Maybe if I was feeling it, I'd wear dress boots instead of my Timberlands. When I was off, I resorted to track pants and sweatshirts to lie around the house in or do my errands.

Tonight, I felt like I should dress business, but at the same time, I didn't think Julian would be dressed up. I finally chose a pair of black slacks and a purple silk blouse. I decided to throw on my gray suede boots instead of wearing heels. He wasn't that tall, so I didn't want to be taller than him. Although being taller than him might be a good idea, maybe give me the upper edge.

I sighed; no, it wouldn't. Somehow, I knew it wouldn't so I grabbed my original choice and pulled them on.

When I finished getting dressed, I let Garda out one last time and grabbed my keys. As I turned around to leave, I glanced back at Garda and said, "Wish me luck," and he gave me one quick bark before I headed out to the garage. It was either a "good luck" or "be careful" bark. I didn't know which one would have fit better at that time.

Tonight, I was feeling a bit spunky, so I decided to take my brand-new Dodge Challenger. It had been a small gift to me after Trevor died. It was something I had always dreamed of having, and I even went as far as to have it painted one of the original Dodge colors, Plum Crazy.

I climbed behind the wheel and turned over the engine. The car sprang to life and the roar that came out from under it was helped by the special exhaust system that had been installed. You can't have a muscle car that doesn't sound like a muscle car. No way!

On my way to the café, I found myself still both oddly nervous and excited. I found a parking spot right away as it was a Monday night and not that busy. I didn't see the Mustang yet, so I told the hostess I was meeting someone and went to wait at the bar.

After ordering a chocolate martini, I drank about half of it before I felt eyes on the back of my neck. My body stiffened as the scent of cinnamon reached my sensitive nose. With all the smells of the food in the establishment, it was a wonder that I could pick up on the slight tang in the air. A smile crossed my lips quickly before I was able to control it and erase it from my face.

I felt Julian getting closer, and when he sat down next to me, the heat radiated off of him. I turned and stopped breathing. My God! This man's eyes were to die for! I tried to keep the expression off my face, but I was not sure I was able to, since he gave me a lopsided grin. I picked up my glass and threw back the rest of my martini before I gave him my attention again.

Oh, shit! This man was turning my hormones upside down just sitting next to me. How the hell was I going to talk business with him when all I wanted to do was look into his incredible eyes and kiss his gorgeous mouth?

He chuckled next to me. *Okay, what was so funny?* I thought.

Before I could say anything, he caught the bartender's eye and ordered me another drink while ordering a lager for himself.

I was staring at his profile, eyeing his strong cheekbones and the tilt of his nose. I studied the way his chin moved and how his lips rounded out when he spoke. I even went so far as to look right under his ear and watched his pulse beat in the vein. I was enthralled with this man. I had this unbelievable urge to lick that very spot on his neck.

Damn! I shook my head and stared at the surface of the bar. When I looked back up, I found Julian watching me.

"Evening, Kristin. I like this place." He glanced around. "I hadn't pegged you for a romantic." His smile caused a blush to rise from my neck to my forehead.

Okay, so when all else fails, resort to being sarcastic. "Yeah, well the drinks are good." I reached over for the new martini the bartender set down. I heard Julian chuckle quietly. These drinks were too good, and if I keep this pace up, I'll be crawling out of here and calling a cab. Not that alcohol seemed to affect me. I could drink any man under the table and barely register on a breath test, which was bizarre, and another thing I kept to myself.

When I was able to get the heat under control on my face, I turned back to him and knew I had better start talking business while I still could. It would help me to calm down a little bit, and maybe after talking, I could see him more as a coworker than as this gorgeous hunk of flesh who was staring straight into my eyes and grinning at me. Jesus…I was blushing again.

This is soooo not going right, I thought.

I heard that voice again. *"Oh, I think it is going just fine."*

I watched him for a moment and his smile slowly slid away. "Relax, okay? Just enjoy yourself for a little while. You have no idea how long it has been since I had a smart, beautiful woman as company."

I took a deep breath, not believing a word he just said, but at the same time thinking, *Yeah, well—same here.*

The hostess chose that moment to tell us our table was ready. Julian was right beside me and I felt the palm of his hand land softly on the small of my back as we walked. If I stopped focusing on the hostess for one second, I would have melted down to the floor into a puddle.

The feel of his hand on my back sent shivers of delight through my body. I focused on the hostess and on putting one foot in front of the other. Finally, we reached our table, a small two top at the back of the restaurant. Could we possibly have gotten any more of a cozy table?

"Yeah, it could be cozier if we were sitting on a couch in front of a fire," I heard the masculine voice inside my head say softly. Okay. Where the hell was this stuff coming from?

Julian held out my chair and I stared at him for a long moment, wondering if he would pull it out from underneath me when I sat. "Sit, Kristin," he said, and shook his head.

A sense of déjà vu hit me, and I grabbed the edge of the table as my head spun.

"You okay, Kristin?" he asked, seemingly concerned.

"What? Oh, yeah. I'm fine. Just had a strange feeling, but I seem to be getting a lot of those these days." I gave him a tight-lipped smile and picked up my menu to hide behind and pull myself together.

We spent the next few minutes figuring out what we were going to order. He asked me if the steaks were any good and I said only if you get them nice and rare. An eyebrow rose over his sexy eyes. "Just the way I like them."

After commenting on the steaks, I got this undeniable urge to have just that, a nice, juicy, and barely warm hunk of meat. Why I suddenly liked rare meat, I didn't know. Maybe I was lacking in iron or something and it was my body's way of letting me know it needed something.

We both ended up ordering steaks and sat gazing at each other over the small table for a few moments. I cleared my throat. Okay, we needed to talk business, and I had to stop staring at him. I felt like a freaking teenager in front of a heartthrob rock star.

"So, Julian, would you like to start answering my questions now?" I cocked my head to the side as I spoke.

"Sure, what do you want to know? Where I grew up? How old I am? Where I live?" He said all this with a serious face.

"Funny, Julian—funny." I shook my head and wondered if I was going to find anything out from him tonight. "The case, the girl who died, the Taylors—you remember them, don't you?"

He contemplated for a moment and finally said, "Okay, if we talk business for a little while, will you relax and try to enjoy yourself? I want to get to know you better."

Why? That was the first thing I wanted to ask, but I held my tongue. "Fine, if that will get you to talk to me about the case, then fine." I sighed. Not that I even remotely wanted to talk about myself, but if I could get him to talk business, I would find a way to get out of talking about myself later.

He smiled and said, "Okay, good." He reached out and took a drink from his beer. I watched the movement of his hand. *Nice, strong, masculine hand like in my dream,* I thought. As if knowing I was looking at his hand, he reached across the table and put his on top of mine.

It was like being shocked. Like an electrical impulse ran right up my arm and through my entire body. I gasped and found in his eyes that he was feeling the same surprise. *Oh, hell.*

When I was able to move again, I pulled my hand away, breaking the current that ran between us, although I could still feel it coursing through every nerve ending.

"Julian, if you keep that up, we aren't going to get any talking done —or eating, either, I might add." I cleared my throat again, shifted in my seat, and couldn't believe that I actually said the next sentence that went through my head. "If you don't stop staring at me like that, I'm going to grab your arm, and drag you out of this place." At that moment, I was being drop-dead serious.

I wasn't thinking about the case, or the food, or even the romantic atmosphere. Right then, the only thing I could think about was putting my hands all over his body, kissing his lips, feeling my breasts push up against his chest. Forget work! Forget the fucking case! Forget how many people had been killed—right now, I just wanted to feel alive, and I wanted him to make me feel that way.

"Then let's go." He looked me dead in the eyes as he said it. Another sense of déjà vu flooded my mind. Our eyes stayed locked together. My body felt as if it was slowly burning from the inside out. When I didn't answer him, he looked over his shoulder impatiently for the waitress.

As if knowing she was about to be needed, our server appeared right beside us. "Is there a problem?" she asked, looking at Julian.

"No, ma'am, no problem, but we just found out we need to be someplace else. Could you possibly make those orders to go?" He smiled up to the waitress, who seemed to be as drawn to his eyes as I was.

"Sure, they were just getting your orders completed. I'll have them packed up. I'll bring the bill right over." She hurried away.

We sat in silence. The only words shared were through eye contact. A cloud of sexual tension hung in the air around us. I was trying not to picture what I wanted to do to him or what I wanted him to do to me, but it was useless. My body was vibrating with a need that I somehow knew he could fulfill.

When the waitress reappeared a couple of minutes later, she had our orders packaged in a fancy take-out bag and handed Julian the check. He pulled out his wallet, took two one hundred-dollar bills and stuck them into the black vinyl checkbook without even looking at the bill.

Are you kidding me? I know the bill was probably only sixty-five dollars tops, with the drinks included. Who drops a hundred plus for a tip?

Before I could change my mind, Julian stood beside me and pulled my chair out. He put his hand on my back again and led me out of the restaurant. Currents of heat tore through every inch of my body.

His 1968 midnight-blue Mustang sat under a large parking light. I was in awe of this vehicle as he guided me toward it. It was the car I had dreamed of over and over again, and as I approached it, I wanted to replay the dream right then, right there.

He unlocked the door and pulled it open, setting the take-out bag in the back. I stood beside him watching him, waiting. He turned and our gazes collided, he stepped closer. I emptied my lungs slowly, staring into his jeweled eyes as my knees quivered.

Over his shoulder, I saw a man staring at us, but right that second, I didn't want to think about any other man. I only wanted to think about this man, this incredibly sexy man with eyes like rich gemstones, who was moving toward my lips.

I could smell his breath; cinnamon filled my senses and I stopped breathing again. My eyes half closed, waiting in anticipation. In the back of my mind, I heard footsteps, but they didn't matter to me.

As Julian put his lips to mine, my life seemed to flash before my eyes. Bits and pieces of things that had happened to me, and things that I thought had happened, but I couldn't exactly remember. It was as if my heart and soul had known this man before, as if they had joined like this in a past life.

The kiss was gentle, but after only a few seconds, our bodies fell against each other and we were holding on for dear life. *Oh my God…*

When we separated, he continued to assault my senses with gentle kisses to my cheeks and jaw line. I felt him kiss the side of my neck and nuzzle it slightly, his lips teasing the vein under my ear. My eyes were barely open; I was in heaven.

Then two small sentences were spoken that would forever change my life.

First, Julian whispered something in my ear. "My God, I missed you so much, Calista." The words poured ice water right through my burning veins. I began to pull back when I realized it wasn't my imagination.

At that same moment when I was pulling back, I heard another man's voice off to the right, a voice that set me on edge instantly. "So, Jules, when the hell were you going to tell me Calista was alive?" He sounded pissed, and my feet shifted me out of Julian's reach without thought.

Julian's body tensed, before he snapped his neck around faster than I would have thought possible. Julian literally snarled at the man as a feral gleam took over his eyes, and it reminded me of a rabid animal. He turned completely, blocking me from the stranger.

They stared each other down for a long time. I waited for someone to speak, but neither one said anything. When I couldn't stand the silent tension, I stepped around Julian and studied the man, narrowing my eyes, and said, "Who the hell are you?"

He didn't answer me. But when his eyes scanned over my body from the tips of my boots to the top of my head, I couldn't move. His bright emerald eyes seemed to glow in the darkness of the night. He was breathtaking, and silent. So silent, that I grew uncomfortable at the way he caressed me with his eyes. I spun around to close myself off from his scrutiny and faced Julian. "Who the hell is Calista?"

CHAPTER SIXTEEN

JULIAN

*I*t was already late afternoon when I woke. The first thing I did when I opened my eyes was reach for my phone. Two voice messages and a couple of e-mails. Checking the voicemails hastily, I found that Alexander and Gabriel had both called. Not who I was hoping for, and I quickly decided I would call them both back later.

I opened my e-mail and found the response that I wanted, the one from Kristin. It was brief, stating only a time and place for our meeting. At least she hadn't said no. I climbed out of bed with a smile on my face and a feeling of anticipation that I had not felt in years.

When I got downstairs to the kitchen, I took out a bag of blood and warmed it before calling Gabe back. He was only checking in and stated that it had been quiet around the Taylors. I told him when and where I was meeting Kristin and suggested he stay with the Taylors just in case Damon showed up tonight. I told him I would meet with him later tonight or tomorrow to discuss what we would do next.

I was looking at the phone trying to figure out if I should call Alexander or not. I wasn't ready to tell him about the whole Calista-Kristin issue yet. I didn't have too much to offer in the way of more information on the case and decided that I would hold off until after I had spoken to Kristin tonight. There was no doubt he was going to be pissed off that I was ignoring him, but I didn't care.

Before I got ready to go, I Googled the Riverwood Café to see what type of a place she'd chosen for our meeting. The pictures displayed a quaint and cozy atmosphere. It was very close to what I would have chosen for the night.

After I was dressed and on my way to meet Kristin, my phone rang and I pulled it out of the pocket of my leather jacket thinking it might be her, but when I saw it was Alex, I put the phone back. I didn't want to deal with him, not yet.

I arrived at exactly seven-thirty and looked around the parking lot. I didn't see her Jeep, so I walked in the double glass front door and caught her scent in the air immediately. She was sitting at the bar drinking a martini of some sort; well, more like gulping it. She was nervous. I didn't need to read her mind to know that.

I smiled at the hostess and pointed at Kristin to let her know I was there to meet with her. She told me our table would be ready soon. I noted the way Kristin had her head tipped back while she held the martini glass and saw just the hint of a smile cross her face as I approached. She knew I was there.

I climbed onto the bar stool next to her and waited for her to turn her head toward me. So many thoughts raced through her mind, and I was fighting hard not to show the pure joy I felt at hearing them. I wasn't totally successful in that as I watched her grab her drink and throw the rest of it back quickly.

When I spoke finally, I never dreamed I would get the reaction I did. The blush that crept up her face so suddenly made me think about the hot blood coursing through her veins, and a quick blast of bloodlust filled me. I grinned at her, not wanting to open my mouth yet, as my teeth had started to elongate as I envisioned sinking them into her warm neck, or better yet, the soft tissue of the inside of her thigh. I mentally groaned and shifted in my seat.

I guided Kristin over to our table in the back. The soft silk of her blouse on my hands reminded me of how her skin would feel. She was fighting her attraction to me. I wasn't going to let that happen.

She told me the steaks were good when they were rare, and I could just imagine how the taste for blood was just now beginning to show its side in her body. It would not be long before she would start to crave it constantly.

I was so enthralled with watching her and dipping into her thoughts. We eventually made a deal that we would talk business for a few minutes, before we moved on to a more relaxed conversation.

Just after we made this deal, I reached for my beer and found Kristin studying my hand intently. I placed the glass back on the table while listening in on her mind. She had dreamed of me? I reached for her, no longer able to hold back as I wished I could ask her about them.

The current that blasted through us brought the memories of our life together alive in an instant. I couldn't look away, and it was as if I was standing in Night Crawlers all over again, telling her I wanted to grab her and run.

We couldn't get out of there fast enough. I was tempted to throw money on the table and say forget the food, but it came at the last second. I pulled out Kristin's chair, rested my hand on her back, and felt her body quaking under my fingertips.

I didn't know where her Jeep was so I walked her over to my Mustang. She was eyeing it intently. We didn't speak as we approached it, and I pulled my keys from my jacket, unlocking the passenger door. I set the bag of food in the back seat and turned to move past her, only I never got that far.

She was so close, and her sweet scent grabbed hold of me like a vise around my heart. I thought of nothing else as I took a step closer to her, leaning down to touch my lips to hers. Within a second, the galaxy exploded again, and I grabbed her to me, kissing her with such intensity that I felt as if my body would explode here in the parking lot.

We pulled back and I could not stop myself from spreading kisses over her face and the side of her neck. I felt the heat of her blood pulsing against my lips. The overwhelming memories slammed back into me so fast that I forgot about all the pain of the past and whispered softly, "My God, I missed you so much, Calista."

Those words, at that very moment, changed everything. She drew in a sharp breath and I realized my mistake immediately, but not before Alex interrupted.

"So, Jules, when the hell were you going to tell me Calista was alive?" He wasn't just angry; he was livid. I heard it burning in his voice and saw it shimmering in his eyes as I spun around. I instinctively put myself in front of Kristin protectively.

Kristin looked over my shoulder and said, "Who the hell are you?" She pushed past me. Alex had her in his sights and he was inspecting every inch of her. In the distance, I could hear traffic on the road, but around us it was deadly silent. Alex had not said a word and I felt Kristin spinning through a variety of emotions. None of them bothered me as much as the attraction one she latched on to for a moment. I winced as she spun around to face me. "Who the hell is Calista?"

I couldn't speak, couldn't come up with any words at that moment.

"You haven't told her, Julian?" Alex sneered at me. Then he turned his attention back to Kristin. She was regarding Alex carefully, and looking as if she wanted to either hit something or run.

"Told me what?" she said through clenched teeth.

I finally found my voice, and ignoring her, I spoke to Alex. "No, Master Alexander, I didn't have the time," I said with steel in my voice.

Kristin's face flipped back and forth. "Master Alexander? Julian, who the hell is this guy?" She pointed at Alex. I felt the anger preparing to burst from her body.

Alex ignored her and stared daggers into me. "But you have the time to coerce her into your bed, like you are oh-so-damn-good-at, Julian."

I peered at Kristin and saw her eyes widen. Her thoughts moved too quickly for me to latch on to. What I was able to see was her eye color switching from bright-blue to steel-gray.

The words that Alex said were meant to cut her to the quick, and they did. She looked as though someone had just slapped her, and she took a step away from us.

She clearly didn't understand what he meant, making it sound as if I tried to get every woman I met into my bed. She took another step back, shaking her head.

Turning to Alex, she looked at him and told him, "I don't know who the hell you are, or who this Calista person is, but thank you."

Did she just thank him? Thank him for what? I wanted to grab her, make her stop and tell her she shouldn't be thanking him, but that she should be running from him instead.

She faced me again. "Stay away from me, Julian." She turned and walked briskly over to a car parked in a darker area of the lot. There were several SUVs parked over that way, so I didn't see what kind of car she got into, but from the rumble of it, I was not entirely surprised. It seemed to go with her mood, growling as it came to life.

I saw the reflection of red on the trees behind her as she threw the car into reverse and backed out enough to give her space to go the other way in the lot, away from us, away from me. It wasn't until she drove around a corner that I saw it was a dark purple-colored Dodge Challenger. I wanted to run after her, but I turned to Alex with hatred in my eyes.

"What are you doing here, Alex?" I asked heatedly.

"You didn't answer my calls." He glared back at me.

"If I'd had something to tell you, I would have called you," I told him. "Why are you here?" I asked him again.

"Working the case and being more productive than you, it seems—at least with the case; I'm not talking about the ladies." He leered at me.

"You had no right to come here, Alex, and you had no right to speak to her," I said, trying to calm myself down.

"No right to speak to her?" He took two steps closer. "Why shouldn't I speak to her? She was to be my mate before you stole her away from me. I loved her and you came behind my back and tricked her into bed with you!" He was yelling at this point and two people who were exiting the restaurant stopped to observe the drama, probably wondering if they should call the police or go back inside until it was safe.

"Alex, you never allowed me to explain what happened. Shit, you never even allowed Calista to explain it to you. You just stomped out and refused to speak to either one of us."

"Julian, it means nothing now, that is the past." He shook his head, hands on his hips, looking at the ground. "We need to focus on what's happening now." He lifted his chin to eye me carefully.

I waited.

"Go back to the house. I'll be back there later. We will discuss the case then," he said abruptly.

"Is that an order, Master Alexander?" I narrowed my eyes.

"Julian, I don't want to order you to do anything," he said, lowering his voice. "But I want you to stay away from that woman tonight. So yeah, it's an order."

"Her name is Kristin, Alex. Not *that woman*—Kristin." I turned away from him, knowing I could not disobey him. I climbed into the Mustang, slammed the door, and headed back to the VMF house. I was angry at myself, furious at Alex, and terrified that with Alex here, I might lose the one thing that I wanted back more than anything else in life.

Her.

CHAPTER SEVENTEEN

KRISTIN

I was angry. No, I was beyond fucking furious, and totally annoyed with myself for wanting Julian so much that I had fallen into some stupid testosterone trap. He was a freaking playboy, of course he was! I had no idea who that other man was. But it was so obvious that there was major animosity between the two men. Julian had called him Master Alexander, was Master his first name?

I had fled from the parking lot. I was pissed and mortified to have fallen into that lust-covered trap. When something like that happened, it was either fight or flight—that was how I was wired.

I could have stayed and fought for something that I knew nothing about—or run like hell. I ran. I sped away in my Challenger, wanting to drive like hell from whatever it was I left back there, but I needed to focus and go straight home.

I flipped my blinker on to make a turn. What power did Julian hold over me that could take away all sense of reason and have me panting in heat with only one intense smoldering gaze? How could I have come so unglued standing in a damn parking lot? And how dare that Alex guy come along and break it up!

Wait! That guy stopped it from going further. I thanked him. That was the right thing to do, right? Jesus, what the hell was going on in my life all of a sudden? A woman dies. There are others who have recently died in the same mysterious way. Several very handsome and sexy men come into town claiming to be some kind of security, and then I fall in complete lust with a guy who supposedly drags all his women straight to bed. A very angry and strangely handsome man steps in and breaks through the hazy lust bubble I'd been in, and wham! Here I am…running from who knows what.

Shit! I cranked the music up so loudly that I couldn't think and focused on the rest of the drive home.

I let Garda out and went to my bedroom to strip out of my clothes. The scent of cinnamon surrounded me as I lifted my shirt over my head and I winced—Julian. I tossed the shirt angrily into the hamper. As I waited for the water to warm, I realized I could still smell him on my skin. A residual quiver of need ran through my stomach as the smell brought back the arousing feelings that he had brought out in me. The memory of the touch of his lips on my neck made me gasp while the thought of his hands sliding down over my silk shirt left me clenching my eyes. I threw back the shower curtain and stepped in, immediately grabbing the liquid soap and washing the scent away. I had to get him off of me.

As I washed my hair, I tried to fight back the feeling of loneliness that threatened to engulf me. Tears prickled at the back of my eyelids. Why the hell was I feeling this way? Was it because a few minutes ago I had been in the arms of a man who made my heart race? Because it had been so long since I had been held or loved, and I wanted—needed—it so much? Or was it because I now found myself in a situation that seemed so damn familiar, yet made absolutely no sense.

With track pants and a sweatshirt on, I made my way back to the kitchen. Garda was sitting patiently outside the back door, so I let him in before pouring a glass of wine. He followed me into the living room and lay down near my glider as I turned on the stereo and picked out a CD with mellow music. I needed to relax, and this classical piano CD was the perfect one for just that.

I slipped back and forth in the glider as I sipped from my wine glass. Now that I had some peace and quiet, and I had calmed down, it was time to think about what happened tonight. Did I imagine the chemistry with Julian? Could I be so love-starved that I made up the feelings I saw radiating from his eyes? Who was that guy, Master Alexander? There had been so much tension between the two men, a tension that made no sense, but yet, somehow it did. The biggest question that came to mind was who is this Calista woman that they both mentioned?

I decided to start with the new man, Alex. I knew very little about him, so he would be easy to contemplate quickly. I had only stood in front of him for a few moments, but I gathered quickly that he was all business. I closed my eyes to recall the image of him in a dark charcoal suit, light blue shirt, and black dress shoes. Every inch of him alluded to being a man of control and power. Was he Julian's boss?

He was tall, maybe six foot two or so, with wavy brown hair that fell to his shoulders. The lighting from the overhead parking lot light had thrown shadows on his face, making it look unforgiving. I got the immediate sense that he was very attractive but didn't remember much more of him from the few moments I was in his presence. Garda sat up quickly, my eyes flipped open, and I heard a car pull up in front of my house. I dropped my head back against the cushion. *I don't want company right now,* I thought as I groaned. I just wanted to dwell on everything for a few minutes, and drink enough to fall into a deep sleep. I tried to listen to the engine to see if it was a car I recognized, but it didn't fit any that I could picture.

Sighing loudly, I went to the front door. I could hear soft footsteps coming up the steps. I flipped on the outside light and pulled open the door at the same time. On the other side of the storm door was the Alexander guy. I stumbled back a step with surprise. How the hell did he know where I lived?

He stood quietly, watching, waiting for me to say something. Outside my front door, you had to take a large step up to enter into my house. So from where he stood, we were almost the same height. I contemplated him for a moment before I pushed open the storm door. "What do you want?"

"Kristin, I am very sorry about earlier. My name is Alexander Armstrong." He spoke quietly, with a deep, sexy, authoritative voice that made me want to fall to my knees. He paused for a moment, and then continued. "I also apologize for bothering you in your home, but I think we have many things to discuss."

"I don't know about that." I eyed him suspiciously. "What do you think we have to talk about?" If he said Julian, I would slam the door in his face.

"Not Julian," he said, as if knowing what just passed through my mind. "I'd like to talk to you about the case you are working on, the case with the Taylors. I believe there is some information we need to share with each other." I fought the shiver that threatened to overtake my body at the sound of his voice. Jesus, what was with these men?

"What makes you think there's information that we should share?" I kept my voice hard, dredging up the feelings of anger from earlier to keep it tight and unemotional.

He flexed his jaw from side to side. "Kristin, believe it or not, we are working on the same case, and we are on the same team here."

I snorted. "Yeah, okay. How is it that a security company—and I assume you work for this VMF—and my police department have any connection with the homicide of a young woman?"

He put his hands on his hips and hung his head for a moment. "There is more of a connection than you realize. Please, let me come in and we can talk."

I thought for a moment. I had no idea who this man was, but if he did have information that could help solve my case, wouldn't it be worth a few minutes to discuss it? "Are you willing to answer some other questions?" I asked him.

I watched his shoulders and chest rise as he inhaled deeply. "As best as I can, I promise."

I gave him a brief nod and opened the storm door. "Come on in." Garda regarded him carefully before taking a sniff of his legs. He seemed satisfied with the results and walked into the living room to lie back down in the center of the space. His head rested on his big front paws with his eyes and ears on high alert.

I turned back to Alexander after Garda was situated. I stepped back so that it was easier to see his face. I hadn't realized how tall he was, more like six foot four. He had green eyes, like deep rich emeralds.

"Can I get you a glass of wine?" I asked as I put more distance between us.

"That would be very nice, thank you." His lips were full, and his jaw was no longer clenched and tense.

"Take a seat in the living room, I'll be right back." I went into the kitchen and poured him a glass with shaky hands. When I entered the living room, I found Alexander standing in front of my television stand looking at a picture.

"Who is this man with you?" he asked, his voice deeper and huskier than I'd heard it.

"My husband, Trevor." I placed his wine on top of a ceramic coaster on the glass coffee table. His back seemed stiff when I turned around and saw him still staring at the picture.

"You're married?" he asked in the same tone.

"I was." I sighed. "Trevor was killed in the line of duty two years ago when he was trying to apprehend a suspect. He was actually shot in the crossfire, by one of his own guys." I'd had long enough to deal with the grief from that. I could now say it without feeling the pain I had once felt.

"Do you have children?" He asked so softly I almost did not hear him. His shoulders and back seemed so tense that they looked like they could snap at any second.

"No. No, we were too wrapped up in our careers to want kids." His shoulders visibly relaxed. "Maybe if he had lived…" I said softly. I was standing slightly behind him looking at the picture of Trevor and I, when Alex turned toward me.

I caught the strong scent of spices and coffee coming from him. It was a nice smell, and I tilted my head back to look into his face.

"Good." The expression on his face confused me; it held tenderness and relief. He continued when he realized his word choice was rather rude. "I mean, it's good that you don't have children who are missing a father." He was observing me closely.

I realized then how absolutely gorgeous this man was. The strong features of his face spoke volumes, the way his nose was so straight, and his chin seemed to match it so perfectly, as if an artist had carved him from stone as a God. He could have stepped out of a GQ advertisement. His eyes were a deep, dark emerald green that glowed with warmth as he looked down at me. His unique scent twisted around me, and I found myself intoxicated by it.

He reached out slowly, running a finger from my cheekbone down to my chin. "My God, how much you look like her," he whispered, with absolute awe in his eyes.

I was enthralled at the way he studied me and realized how easy it would be to step forward and ease up on my toes to put my lips to his.

Oh, hell no…what was I thinking!

I blinked and stepped out of reach. Was I so sexually frustrated that I would throw myself at not only one man tonight, but two?

I turned away and sank down in my glider, putting as much distance between us as possible and allowing my shaking legs to gain control. I took a deep gulp of my wine and held the almost empty glass between my two hands.

Alexander moved over to the couch, shrugging out of his suit jacket. I watched as he tossed it over the back of my couch, noting the way the muscles under his dress shirt flexed with the material. He sat and took a sip from his glass. His shirt looked as if it was made of silk, and my fingertips tingled at the thought of running them over the material. The shirt was open at the collar; smooth skin visible in the V of the shirt. What would that skin feel like under my fingertips? Oh, good Lord! I looked down at my drink wishing I had the bottle in front of me.

I took a moment to gain control of myself and finally asked him, "Who is Calista? That is the 'her' you are referring to, isn't it?" I didn't raise my eyes from my glass.

I heard him draw in a deep, calming breath. Was he nervous? "She is a woman from a long time ago. Someone that Julian and I both loved very much." His voice echoed pain and loneliness, something I could relate to, and I lifted my eyes to his and got lost for a moment. "You look so much like her," he said quietly. There was an intense heat in his voice and the color of his eyes seemed to brighten even more. I bit my lip trying to control the urges inside of me.

Maybe she was a relative of mine. Maybe I had a twin sister whom I didn't know about.

"No," he stated as if knowing what I was thinking. "She was an only child."

My eyes were called "mirrored" because they reflected my emotions, but did they really speak those kinds of volumes? Was there enough visible in them for him to know exactly what I'd been thinking?

"How did you know I was thinking that?" I asked him carefully.

"Kristin, there is so much you don't know. I don't know where to even start." He shook his head slowly, staring at the crystal glass in front of him.

"How about from the beginning," I replied. He toyed with the stem of his wine glass, with long, lean fingers that looked as if they would be so gentle and warm against my skin. God, I had to stop thinking like this.

He lifted his head and the left side of his lip was up in a partial smile, or maybe it was a smirk. He cleared his throat as if he would speak but turned his attention back to his glass instead.

"Alex, please. I'm not sure what is going on, but things have gotten so strange, and I don't understand any of it," I almost pleaded. I felt more lost than ever right that minute and somewhere inside of me, I knew that this man could give me answers.

"Okay, let's start by saying there is a whole different world out there than the one you are used to. One where the normal person would have trouble imagining what it is actually like. You have grown up in a different way than us, and some things will be hard for you to completely understand right now." He watched me closely while he spoke.

"Okay...so what are we talking about here, a cult of some kind?" What he told me didn't actually tell me anything; it only gave me more questions.

"More like a breed," he said.

"A *breed?*" I snorted. "What are you talking about?" Was this guy nuts? Where was my off-duty weapon? Maybe I should have gotten that before I let him in. A breed, were we talking nationality here? He looked American enough to me.

"Yes, a breed. There are people who are different, and they are mixed around the general population—hidden to the human eye, for the most part. They pretend to be part of your society, but they are actually something else entirely. The Taylors are examples of that, as are Julian, Gabriel, and me."

Okay, I was now officially drowning in a pool of uncertainty. What the hell was he talking about? I glanced around the room as if I would get an answer from someplace there. When I didn't, I returned my gaze to him and said, "Yeah, okay...well, you all look normal enough to me."

"Yes, we do look normal for the most part; we make ourselves fit in. It is because of our difference, though, that people are dying."

Okay, now we're talking. The dying part brought me back to reality. "You mean like Dawn Taylor and the four people in Springtown who died last week?" I raised a questioning brow at him.

He seemed surprised that I knew about the others. "Yes, like them. What do you know about those other ones?"

"I know that four females died: two mothers and two daughters. That they had their throats torn out, not cut, but torn out like Dawn's was. I also know that they had wounds to their chests above their hearts, although Dawn did not. I don't know much more than that. The evidence at the scenes has been almost nonexistent when it comes to the suspect. The only things found were items belonging to the victims. What do *you know* about this, Alex?"

It felt good to be talking shop now. I always felt better, more in control, when I talked about work and avoided feelings and emotions.

A strange expression crossed his face, something almost like pride. "Those females all died because of what they were. The person who killed them is trying to stop our breed, to put an end to it forever. He does this by killing our women. Sometimes just before they mate, sometimes it's when they are older or after a child is born to them."

"That's pretty sick," I said sadly, and set my empty glass down on the table next to me.

"He thinks that if he can kill the women and children, then the men will no longer be able to mate, and our breed will die."

I took in his words and considered them for a minute. It made sense if I could actually wrap my head around it all. I was used to sick people trying to ruin others by hurting and stealing from them. I saw it every day in my job.

"What's his name?" I asked.

"Damon," he replied.

Damon. The name alone sounded evil. Okay, so I was finally getting someplace now. I might actually have a lead that could help solve the case.

"Alex, do you know him? Do you know what he looks like?" I could feel excitement flourishing in my body. "If you do, I could get this information out to other officers and we could locate him." I stood waiting for his answer, ready to move as soon as I had the information.

"Yes, I know him, but I'm not going to tell you any more about him." He stood then, too.

"Oh yes, you are! If you know anything else about him, you need to tell me so that we can find him." I'd taken a couple of steps closer to him without even realizing it, placing my hands on my hips. The intense professional voice was coming out of me, the one I used when I was letting the bad guy know I wasn't playing any games.

"Kristin, no—I'm not." He shook his head. "This is not your battle to fight. It is the responsibility of the VMF to find him and take him out." He started to raise his voice and approached me.

"Like hell! Not my responsibility? What the hell are you talking about? Of course, it's my responsibility. He has killed people; I'm a cop. It's my job to stop people when they do that kind of thing, to put them behind bars where they belong." My voice kept rising as I spoke. "And what makes you think that a security company like yours could take on a serial killer?"

I knew my eyes were steel-gray now. I was pissed. Angry that Alex wasn't taking this seriously and thought his company should take care of it. I eyeballed him, trying to keep my breathing under control as the adrenaline rushed through my body.

Alex stepped forward and looked down into my face. "I missed those eyes, so full of spark and life." And with that, he bent down and kissed me, pulling me tightly into his arms.

Holy—shit! Maybe it was the excitement of knowing I was one step closer to catching the guy who had killed so many people. Maybe it was the wine on top of the two martinis that I'd had earlier without any food and my body was reacting to it for the first time ever. Maybe it was just the heat of the moment and the anger that I had inside. Or maybe it was just because I was crazy, but at that moment, I wanted— no, needed—to kiss him back.

I leaned into him and wrapped one arm around his back and put my other hand on the back of his neck, pulling him closer as I stepped up on my tiptoes and pushed my breasts against his hard chest.

His arms were so strong, and I felt protected within their shelter. His kiss was intense, not the soul burning that Julian's had been, but hot enough to take my breath away. Hot enough to make me want more.

Alexander seemed to come back to earth before I did and ended the kiss. He gently unhooked my hand from his neck, taking both of them in his and putting them against his chest as he spoke.

"Kristin, I am going to do everything in my power to protect you. I am not going to allow Damon to get near you. I refuse to allow that to happen again." He said this with a venomous tone.

"Again? Wait, Alex—Damon has never been near me, and why would he want to hurt me?" I stepped back but kept my hands in his.

He held my hands tighter so that I couldn't get any further away and looked deeply into my eyes. "Damon wants you dead. He killed you once before." He squeezed my hands to his chest, watching my every move. When he heard the sharp intake of breath and saw the questioning in my eyes, he continued. "He killed you because you were—I mean, because you are—a vampire like us."

CHAPTER EIGHTEEN

JULIAN

*A*fter I got into the Mustang, I didn't feel like going back to the house, but knew I needed to do what Alex told me.

In a moment of panic, I realized that Alex was going to go after Kristin. I didn't know where she lived, but he would have found that information out quickly once he heard about her. Yeah, he was probably with her, and jealousy slammed into my gut.

I had been so lost in her, so lost in the memories and the feeling and scent of her that I never even noticed Alex stalking us in the parking lot. I was so intent on her that I failed to allow my senses to fan out and check the area.

What if Alex had been Damon? What if he'd figured it out and had come after her? I'd been so engrossed in my own selfish needs that I'd put her in jeopardy. I closed my eyes, feeling sick. I shuddered thinking again how it could have been Damon and not Alex who walked up on us.

When I pulled in the driveway to the VMF house, I sat in the dark and allowed things to run through my mind. So many memories raced around in there that it made me dizzy. I climbed out of the car and sat on the hood, lying back and looking up at the stars. For the first time in years, I let myself look back on the worst night of my life.

I was at home, our home, standing in the kitchen getting dinner ready, as I knew Calista would be home with Anastasia soon.

Anastasia was our beautiful daughter, with strawberry blond hair that fell in soft curls around her face. She was smart for a five-year-old. I adored her, because she was a miniature of her mother. Full of energy and humor, and she could be so very sneaky.

I glanced at the clock as I heard a car come down the street. We lived in your average neighborhood. A two-story house that sat back off the road, with a long driveway set among growing trees that sheltered our home.

They were right on time, and I was about to walk out the door to welcome them home when I knocked over my wine glass and it fell to the floor. "Damn," I muttered, and grabbed a rag to clean up the mess.

As I bent down, I heard a scream so primal that I ran to the front door as fast as I could. I threw it open with so much force that I almost pulled it off the hinges. Calista stood at the driver's side of the white Pinto she drove. Mail was scattered at her feet. She was screaming "NOOOOOOOOOOOOO..." as she stared over the car's roof to the other side.

On the opposite side of the car stood Damon, and he was holding our limp daughter in his arms. Her throat was already ripped out, blood soaking into her pink coat and dripping onto the ground beneath her.

I examined the scene, frozen, not believing my eyes. I stared at Damon from where I stood rooted in place on the front porch.

Damon sneered at me, fangs long with blood dripping off of them. He dropped Anastasia's body to the ground and jumped at Calista. It had happened so quickly, but it was as if it was happening in slow motion.

As Damon went after her, my body sprang back to life and I started to move. I ran toward him, ran toward Calista. Damon got there before I did; he had been only ten feet away from her, and I was at least fifty feet back. As I approached, I watched him grab her. She was paralyzed by what she just witnessed with Anastasia. She was still screaming, tears coursing down her face. In a strange moment of clarity, I could visualize the drops of salty moisture rolling down her smooth skin. Damon turned her so that she could see me, could watch me come close, but not close enough to save her.

The sound of her skin tearing away as Damon ripped into it with his teeth, pulling at the tendons from one side to the other, was a sound I would

116

never forget. The inside of her neck was totally exposed, her scream cut off by the action.

Her eyes went wide with terror, shock, and then pain. They found mine and I saw the blue fade to gray in that final second. Damon threw her body at me with such force that, as I caught her, I fell backward. Her body landed hard against me and knocked me down.

We landed on the ground and I grasped her tightly, hearing my voice for the first time as I, too, screamed, "NOOOOOOOOO!" Not her, not Calista...NO!

Damon had run but turned to look at me as I lay on the ground holding Calista to my side. Her limp body cradled in my arms, blood seeping into my clothing, into the ground. I looked up at him as he stopped.

"Why, Damon? Why them? Why?" I cried, tears streaking down my face with reckless abandon.

"It's your fault, you know. It's your fault that I do what I do. It will always be your fault, Father." He spat at the ground, spitting out blood, the blood that had come from my wife and my daughter.

Damon turned and disappeared after that, and I didn't have the strength or the power to do anything more than pick Calista up and walk over to Anastasia's body. I fell to the ground, pulling them both into my lap, and cried as I held them both to me. When the police eventually arrived, I was forced to let them go.

As I came back from my private hell, a hell I had lived in for thirty-five years, I found tears rolling down the side of my face into my temples. I was still lying on top of the Mustang. The same Mustang we had first made love on.

What if I had not spilled the wine? What if I had not stopped to clean it up? What if I had not frozen at the door to our home, and had kept running out into the yard? Could I have saved Calista? Could I have saved our daughter?

The what-ifs ran circles in my mind as they had thousands of times since that night, but as I lay there thinking about all of the old what-ifs, I started thinking about new ones.

What if he found out about Kristin? What if I was the one who led him to her? What if he realized who she was and that I loved her and he tried to take her away from me again, this time ending it the way he would have if he'd had time in the past?

Should I stay away from Kristin? Could I protect her? I had failed so many years ago, would I be able to do it now? Would I be able to deal with the pain if I failed her again?

Fuck! I didn't know what to do. The only thing I did know was that I needed to find Damon and kill him.

I might have been his father. I may have been the one to give him life, and bring him into his transition, but he was not my son. My son died the moment he took the first female life all those years ago.

He was dead to me in my heart, and I vowed again that he would soon be dead in all ways.

CHAPTER NINETEEN

ALEXANDER

*L*ast night, Gabriel called to tell me that they arrived safely and made contact with the Taylors. Being the young person that he was, he felt it necessary to explain in detail all that had transpired from the time they arrived.

At first, I got irritated about the commentary, but when he mentioned how Julian acted strangely around the police officer, and how Gina Marie and Julian thought the police officer was Calista, I began to listen much more intently. I even asked him to repeat the whole conversation, so I could make sure I knew everything.

Gabriel did not know the history of Calista and me. He knew only that she had once been mated to Julian and had died at Damon's hands. Since he didn't know my history with her, he had no reason to leave any of the details out. I didn't tell him that I was coming down. I knew that if I mentioned it, he would tell Julian immediately.

When I got into town early that morning, I stayed at a friend's place, not too far from the VMF house. I didn't want anyone to know I was there, yet. I wanted to check out this police officer on my own. When I called Gabriel back to check in with him about the case, he volunteered the information that Julian and Kristin were meeting for dinner.

It wasn't hard to find the restaurant where they were meeting. I decided it would be best if I stayed quiet and waited outside until they came out. I had no intention of letting Julian see me there. I found a parking spot a little way from Julian's Mustang, and I waited.

I didn't have to wait too long before the left glass door swung outward and a woman dressed in black slacks and a purple blouse exited with Julian right behind her. They walked closely and Julian had his hand on the small of her back, guiding her toward the Mustang.

I stared at her, watching every step she took. She seemed flushed, intent on something. I observed every detail, from the top of her short strawberry blond hair down her thin neck, the shape of her shoulders and waist, the length of her legs and the shade of the gray boots she wore.

A pain tore through my chest as I realized that she did look exactly like Calista. The loneliness that I'd endured for all these years since she'd chosen Julian overwhelmed me. She hadn't known how much I truly loved her, how much I wanted her to become mine. How I wanted to protect her and allow her to grow with me in our world.

I couldn't stop myself now as I stepped out of the car. I watched them as they walked to the Mustang and Julian put a bag in the back seat. I felt the emotion coming off them as I stood there, and I refused to stand back and watch it happen again. As Julian leaned in to kiss her, I felt the heat double as they embraced. I watched the kiss end and heard the words Julian whispered to her; I knew that I was being given a second chance at that very second.

Up close, the woman looked even more like Calista. She was angry and the sparks arcing from her eyes reminded me of our many disagreements in her previous life. We hadn't had major fights, not out of anger, ours were out of passion, and I loved to watch her eyes change color, as they were now. My heart began to beat harder.

Julian had been furious, even more so when I sent him packing back to the house. As much as he wanted to, he would not disobey me. I hated having to pull rank on him. Even after so many years and problems between us, I still thought of him as my best friend.

I had already done enough research to know where the woman lived and I drove over to her house slowly, allowing her some time to calm down, knowing she would probably need it before I arrived and put her life in a tailspin.

My headlights flashed over the front of her ranch home, showing me how neat and tidy it was. It was nothing fancy, just nicely manicured grass and a simple garden out front around a large cement porch. I briefly wondered if there was a man in her life. Would it be too late?

As I approached the front porch, the light flipped on and the inside door opened. She stood there wearing black track pants and a light blue sweatshirt, looking freshly showered. I waited for her to speak.

As I stepped into her house, the soft, sweet scent that was all her wrapped around me, making me dizzy with want. My heart ached to pull her to me, but I held myself in check while her dog inspected me; I willed it to remain calm. He walked away, taking up guard in the middle of the floor, watching us.

I waited in the living room for her to pour me a glass of wine and my eyes zeroed in on a picture on the cabinet. In the picture, she was nestled in the arms of a handsome young man—blond hair, blue eyes, with an intelligent look about him. He held her tightly from behind as she snuggled against him. A bright sunset in the background reflected off a body of water.

I tensed. Was it too late? Had we found her too late to bring her to our side where she belonged? She had been raised as a human and had no knowledge of her true self.

I heard her walk up behind me, but I couldn't tear my eyes away from the man's face until I knew if I was too late. "Do you have kids?" I asked her quietly, my heart stuttering at the implication it could have if she said yes.

A moment of relief and joy filled me when she said no. "Good." I turned to look at her. I felt her emotions changing gears. As she looked up at me, she went from feeling sad to confused.

I could no longer hold back, I needed to touch her, just one time. For so many years, I had denied my feelings for her. Forced myself to forget about her when she mated with Julian, lived with the pain that she would never be mine, and then she was dead. Gone from both of us. It should have brought Julian and I closer together, yet it became an even bigger divider. This woman who stood in front of me was identical to Calista, only with shorter hair. My fingers slipped over her satiny skin, and I felt a need course from her to me. I wanted to pull her into my arms, but I fought it with all my strength. Her emotions swirled, constantly changing. She was confused, scared, yet she felt a connection with me and was embarrassed to feel such a thing. She stepped away, and I allowed it, for now. I threw my suit jacket over the couch and sat down, taking a drink from the sweet mellow wine she'd poured for me.

What was the best way to explain the situation? How did I explain who Calista was and what this case was really about? It was not normal to explain our matters to the humans who lived around us. We kept our business to ourselves when we could. I knew that I had to find a way to quell her curiosity while still keeping her from feeling overwhelmed. Would she believe me? Would she think I was crazy? I tried to explain to her about our breed without coming right out and saying it. I wanted her to get used to the idea that things could be different. See if she would accept that possibility before I gave her more.

She had no interest in the breed itself, but kept her focus on the job she performed. That is where her control came from. She had no control over her emotions, but she could control and analyze things, events, people, but not herself.

She was intelligent and her mind shifted quickly from one thing to another as she processed the information that I gave her. She remained calm until I got to the part about not giving her more. If there had been any doubt that she was Calista before, there was none now as her eyes flashed with anger and determination. I had seen this side of her before, but she had never directed it toward me. That is where Kristin was different from Calista. She showed no fear in talking back to me. She was so headstrong, and I realized I needed to do everything I could to protect her. *We* needed to do everything we could to protect her. I had loved her before but failed to tell her that. This woman in front of me was already claiming a portion of my heart. I loved the passion coming out of her as she fought for her beliefs. I loved it more than I had ever loved her in the past.

No amount of control would have been enough to stop me from taking what I felt was mine. She curled herself around me the moment our lips met. I expected her to fight, or hesitate, but she fell into the kiss as quickly as I did. I felt her heart beating against my chest, could feel the lusty need rising in her as the kiss continued. Her mouth so sweet, so luscious, was more demanding than it had been in the past, and I found I already adored this new woman. There was no doubt that I could have lifted her off the floor and carried her to the bedroom to make love to her. I could have claimed her right then, but I wouldn't do that. I refused to take her choice away. Julian had once done that and had stolen what was mine. As much as I cared about this woman, and craved her, I would not take her choice away from her. I slowly pulled away and unfurled her arms from around my neck, clasping her hands to my chest. It was now or never. "Kristin, I am going to do everything in my power to protect you. I am not going to allow Damon to get near you. I refuse to allow that to happen again," I vowed to her.

"Again? Wait, Alex. Damon has never been near me, and why would he want to hurt me?" She tried to step back, but I held her hands tightly.

"Damon wants you dead. He killed you once before." She went still, her body tense, and the quick gasp told me she had heard me. "He killed you because you were—I mean, because you are—a vampire like us."

CHAPTER TWENTY

KRISTIN

*M*y jaw dropped and I gaped at Alexander. For a few moments, I was stock-still, allowing his words to flow through my brain over and over again, and then I started laughing. I tore my hands from his chest, bent over, and laughed as hard as I had ever laughed before.

I stood, wiping tears from my eyes and gasping for breath, and found Alex watching me closely with a look of total confusion on his face.

"Vampire?" I said between laughs. "Are you insane? A vampire? Yeah, okay." I didn't know what I'd expected him to say, but that sure as hell wasn't it.

He watched me intently, his hands on his hips. Finally, I began to get control over myself; I walked over to the couch and plopped down. Little bubbles of laughter still rolled out of me softly. I wiped the tears from my cheeks. Wow! I hadn't laughed that hard in years. I shook my head, attempting to clear it, and wondered if, somehow, the alcohol had finally affected me.

I focused on Alex and examined him as if I was seeing him for the first time. His dark green eyes glowed with such intensity that they brought a shiver to my body; a handsome strong face, wide shoulders and chest, flat stomach, long muscular legs that pushed against his slacks. He looked like a man, sounded like a man, and sure as hell kissed like one. I would have bet big money that he was "just" a man.

So now that I was no longer laughing and I was examining every inch of him, why did it feel as though what he said made some kind of strange sense? Why did I feel like there was a shred of truth to it? I could read people's body language, and right now his was calm but tense at the same time. Like he was waiting to see what I would do. It didn't seem to be saying, "I just pulled this shit out of my ass."

I scanned the room, searching for an answer that wasn't there. The fight or flight feeling was closing in on me again. My head began to ache. Images popped into it—dreams that once seemed so strange, now almost made sense.

Alex must have sensed my mood change because he moved closer to me with his hands up in front of him, giving me a look that said, "Relax." As he approached, I jumped up quicker than I would have thought possible and went to shove him away.

I was stronger than most women, and although he looked to weigh over two hundred pounds, I figured I could easily push him aside. My hands made contact with his chest and I pushed with everything I had in me. And nothing happened.

Nothing—as in he didn't move. He didn't budge, but he very quickly grabbed both of my wrists with one of his strong hands, putting them in a death grip, while the other went around my waist and pulled me tightly to him. I might have been strong, but he was way stronger, and a trickle of fear wound around my spinal column.

I panted against his chest as my mind raced and stared up into his eyes defiantly while I tried to pull away from him again. With his body this close to me, I couldn't think, couldn't smell anything but him.

"Kristin," he said very quietly. "Kristin, stop fighting me, you will only hurt yourself," he spoke louder.

I stopped fighting him and put my forehead against his chest. I was lost in what was happening in my mind—flashes of memories, of dreams, of feelings so intense that I thought I would pass out. I forced myself to breathe and willed myself to relax.

When I calmed and leaned into him, he let go of the death grip on my wrists and allowed my hands to fall onto his chest. He held me lightly to him, his hands on my shoulders, not wrapped around my waist, and I quickly tried to step out of his grasp, spinning away from him, meaning to run, to put some distance between us—to hide from his words.

Instead, as I twisted, I lost my balance and fell sideways toward the coffee table. I tried to put my arms out to stop myself but only managed to push my arm through the glass top. I felt the side of my head smack the wood with a crack.

I landed on the floor and the last thing I thought was, *I smell blood*, and then everything went black as I heard Garda bark once.

CHAPTER TWENTY-ONE

ALEXANDER

*W*ell, shit…I hadn't expected that. I hadn't expected the hysterical laughter either, but I thought I'd finally calmed her down. Then she had to fall and knock herself out.

"Damn it!" I looked at her lying on the ground and heard a bark and then a low growl from behind me. I turned slowly to make eye contact with her dog.

That is one big damn dog! "It's okay, boy; I'm not going to hurt her," I spoke softly and cautiously stepped closer to Kristin and bent down. I was counting on the dog feeling my own emotion so he would know I wasn't going to hurt her. I didn't want to hurt the dog if I could help it.

The dog walked over to sniff at her arm where the blood was rushing out. He looked at me as if to say, "What are you going to do now?" He cocked his head and studied me.

"Guess I need to fix her up, huh?" I asked the dog, and he gave a quick bark. I scooped Kristin off the floor and started off down the hallway that was off to the left side of the living room. I figured a hallway meant other rooms, and other rooms meant beds.

I looked inside the first door I came to and found an office. Two desks, two computers, two chairs, but only one desk looked to be used on a regular basis. The other one had a thin coat of dust over everything. *That must have been her husband's,* I thought.

I went further down the hall and found a small bedroom that had a double bed in it, a dresser, and some other accessories. It didn't look lived in, probably the guest room.

One more door down the hall and I hit the jackpot. A king-sized bed with lots of pillows pushed up against the cherry wood headboard. The colors of the room were soothing, all different shades of purple. Her scent was very strong in this room, and I filled my lungs completely.

I laid her on the bed and saw two doors off to the right side of the room. The first door I checked was what I wanted. I opened a few cabinets, looking for medical supplies to fix her arm. I lucked out and found a decent-sized medical kit that contained everything I needed.

Carrying it back to the bedroom, I found the dog was lying on the floor next to the bed, head on his paws, eyes watching me.

"She will be as good as new soon, boy." I wanted to reassure the dog, not sure why I cared, but it seemed like the right thing to do.

I made quick work of cleaning up her arm and putting a few stitches in it to hold it shut till it healed. I was going to make her feed from me. I knew that if she did, she would heal much faster than if she tried on her own. I finished off by wrapping it up with some gauze.

I stood back and realized that her clothes had blood and glass on them; I needed to get her changed. I ripped the sweatshirt off of her and tried not to look at her lean, toned body underneath.

In a dresser drawer, I found clean comfortable clothes. I stood over her, my eyes drawn to her face, my heart aching. She looked so much like Calista had, but now as I studied her again, she also looked so very different to me. She was even more beautiful than I could have ever remembered. Her nose was slightly different, and her body was stronger, more toned than Calista's had been. I couldn't help but run my gaze over her breasts and see how full and round they were, her nipples begged to be touched, tasted, loved. I inhaled deeply to contain the excitement growing in my groin and set about pulling the soft cotton nightshirt over her head. After getting her dressed, I forced myself to step away and put the medical supplies back where I found them, instead of climbing on the bed with her. Before I left the bedroom, I turned back to look at the dog. He lifted his head.

"You stay with her. Protect her," I told him.

The dog got up and walked closer to the bed before lying back down.

"Good boy." That was one hell of a trained dog. I grinned and left to go clean up the living room.

While I was picking up the glass and cleaning blood off the floor, I thought back to when I had first met Calista.

I was on an assignment where a female vampire was going around turning people that she had no right to turn. I knew she was in this area and had stopped at a bar hoping to talk to some locals and hear if they knew where she might be.

The inside of the bar was dark, and I found a seat near the back of the U-shaped bar. It was a good seat, one that would give me a chance to watch the people in the room from the sidelines. There were a lot of vampires in the room, and a good number of humans, too. They were both easy for me to spot. The human emotions and thoughts were like listening to the radio. As you turned the dial, you would pick up on the different people as if they were stations.

I tried to tune a lot of it out, but tonight I needed to keep the airwaves open to see if I could pick up Serena's name.

I heard laughter from behind me, a deep heartfelt laugh that was so clear and fresh that it made me smile. I didn't hear the thoughts that came with the laugh, so I knew it had to be a vampire. I glanced over my shoulder and found myself looking at a beautiful woman with long strawberry blond hair sitting at a table with friends.

There were two other women and two men at the table with her. Was she with one of the men? I observed them closely for a few minutes, and while one of the men seemed to be trying to gain her attention, she didn't seem to notice, or maybe she didn't care.

I ordered a beer and checked out the bar. I didn't want to get sidetracked from my job, but her laughter and voice kept drawing my attention. She was a half-breed; not yet mated. She was getting close to her mating and would need to do that soon to complete her transition to become a full vampire.

Although she was only a half-breed right now, she was very good at controlling her mind and her emotions. Some young vampires couldn't do it as well as she seemed to be able to.

After a few minutes more, and several long swigs from my beer bottle, I felt eyes staring at my back. A wave of lust rolled over me quickly, but I knew it wasn't coming from me. I was used to feeling other people's emotions slam into me all the time.

I turned to see who was sending lustful thoughts to someone and my eyes met with hers. She was staring at me, and the emotions were coming from her. Even in the dark, I could see her eyes were green, a playful bright green.

The eye contact startled me, or maybe it was the sensation I had when our eyes made that contact. It was hot, penetrating, and intense. I was tempted to get off the stool and approach her, but I didn't need a complication in my life right now. I turned back to the bar and swallowed another mouthful of my beer.

It wasn't two minutes later that I caught the scent of butter and sugar and saw someone climb onto the bar stool beside me. I turned to check out my new companion and saw the playful green eyes of the woman from the table. She smiled shyly.

"You gonna rip the glass to shreds too after you finish with that label?" She nodded at the beer bottle I held in my hand. I had been peeling the label back while I watched the people around me. I had a hard time sitting still for too long.

I laughed, and her smile grew more confident.

"Can I buy you another one? Looks like you need a new label to torture." I liked her voice, smooth and strong. She gave off the air of confidence and I realized I felt more comfortable with her than I had before with a woman. We sat at the bar, my case all but forgotten, and talked for hours. She was intelligent, witty, and laughed easily at herself and life. As the night went on, I felt myself drawn further and further into her. I could sense she felt the same way.

I knew that if I had wanted to, I could have asked her to leave with me, and she would have said yes. Somehow that didn't seem right. Somewhere in *my mind, I was seeing more than just a good time in bed. For the first time in my long life, I was seeing someone to share my future with, someone to finally mate with for life.*

I was next in line to be the head of the VMF, and I knew that I could not take the decision of who to mate with lightly. The woman I took to be my mate had to stand up to many tests and be strong and willing to stand beside me through a lot of things. I found myself wondering if Calista would be strong enough for that.

While I did not leave with her, I did walk her out to her car. I opened her car door and she stood on her tiptoes and kissed me on the cheek. I watched as she pulled back, but didn't let her get far before I pulled her into my arms and against my body. The kiss had been a searching one for both of us, as if we were trying to see if the small flames we had fanned all evening would be put out with a kiss or if they would evolve into a higher flame. As I kissed her, my body became an inferno, and she was adding fuel to the fire with the need coming from her. She was just as consumed as I was.

Finally, we ended the kiss. We knew there was something there, but neither of us were ready to know more.

I watched her drive away that night and told myself I would be back to learn more about her. I had every intention of getting to know her better and finding out if she could be the one to move forward with me through life.

Over the next year, I made it a point to stop back in her area any time I could. We spent time together, stealing intense kisses when we were near each other, and talking about everything we could think of.

We never spoke of sleeping together, and I never told her my thoughts of mating with her. I know now that I should have. I knew what she had been feeling. I knew that she would have said yes, she wanted me, but I made the mistake of waiting too long. I allowed business to hold me back and my own fear to keep the words and my wishes inside of me.

As I thought about the past, I carried the coffee table outside and deposited it near her garbage cans sat. I'd make sure to have a new one delivered to her house shortly, one that didn't have glass on top of it.

When I was sure that I had cleaned everything, I stopped once again in front of the TV cabinet, looking at the picture of her and her husband smiling, him standing with his arms wrapped around her, someplace in the warm sunset. A stab of jealousy ran through my body again at the look of happiness on her face.

Back in the bedroom, I found that Kristin had just begun to move around. I sat on the side of the bed and touched her cheek, waiting for her to open her eyes.

This time, I wouldn't wait to tell her. This time, I wouldn't make the mistakes I had made in the past. This time, I would tell her how I felt before it was too late.

CHAPTER TWENTY-TWO

KRISTIN

I don't know how much time passed while I was blacked out and part of me wanted to stay in the darkness. I didn't want to come forward to face what I'd been told. I heard a soft sound next to me as the bed tipped and someone touched me gently on my face. The scent of spices and coffee drifted around me.

"Kristin—wake up, Kristin. I need you to wake up and look at me." It was Alex, and he sounded worried.

I took another second to figure out what had happened. We had been talking—I had gotten angry, or was it that I had gotten scared? I tried to get out of his hold, and I had fallen.

I remembered the shattering of the glass, and the sound of my head making contact with the wood of the table. My arm—my arm had gone through the glass. I tried to move my arm and winced.

"Kristin, hold still. I don't want you to move your arm yet. It's not healed or stitched together very well. You lost a lot of blood." He spoke quietly and I felt his breath wash over my face, bringing his scent up close and personal.

"Kristin, open your eyes, look at me," he pleaded.

I did as he asked. In front of me was his beautiful face, eyes intent on mine, worry or maybe fear filling them. They were so green, and I wanted to get lost in them. I wanted to reach out and touch his face, but I felt so oddly weak.

"Alex—" I said almost breathlessly. "I'm sorry." I closed my eyes again.

"There is nothing to be sorry for." He brushed his fingertips over my cheek. A sigh escaped from my lips and I nuzzled into his palm, needing to feel his touch.

"Kristin, you lost a lot of blood. I want you to take some of mine," he said quietly. "It will help you heal."

With that, my eyes flashed open and I gaped at him. "You're kidding, right? You want me to drink your blood?" I felt a bubble of hysteria growing inside my chest again. What he told me before I fell all came rushing back to me.

"No. I'm not kidding. You are a vampire, Kristin, although you haven't completed your transition. You are close to doing that, and it would be easier for you if you started putting my blood into your body now."

He was speaking as if he actually believed everything he was saying. Where was my gun? I wanted to move away from him. I didn't want to believe him. And yet, a part of me *did* believe him, wanted it to be true. What the hell was wrong with me? Did I hit my head harder than I thought?

Did they exist? Could I be one of them? Could that be why I never truly felt whole? Why I always felt alone?

"My blood is very strong, one of the strongest you could have. It will help you heal quickly," he said quietly.

"Oh my God…" I gulped down the panic rising. "I don't know what to believe. I feel like I'm in a dream and I should be waking up at any time."

"Kristin, if this is just a dream, then follow it. It won't make any difference if this is just a dream, right?" He studied my face for another second. "Haven't you ever dreamed you had bitten someone? That you had drunk from someone before?"

Should I tell him the truth? Could I even admit it out loud?

"Yes." But there was no way I was going to tell him that it had been Julian I dreamed about.

"And in your dream, did you enjoy it?" he asked tenderly, putting his fingers on my chin and holding my face still as I tried to look away from him.

Since I couldn't, I hid behind my eyelids, embarrassed to admit it. "Yes."

"Kristin do not be upset about it. You were dreaming about it because it is your nature. I bet you have had a lot of dreams, and they will all start to make sense now." His gentle voice lulled me into a sense of security, and I opened my eyes. The features of his face had softened, and the touch of a smile graced his lips.

I glanced around the room and realized I was lying in my bed. The soft glow in the room came from a candle on the nightstand. The atmosphere in the room had changed. No longer was the tension thick, but desire was filling the space in the light of the flicker from the wick. The pain in my arm and my head were still very real, but both were taking a backseat to a new feeling, one that began in my throat. No! This was crazy! It couldn't be true.

I looked down at my arm, seeing the white dressing over the injury, I realized with a start that I was wearing a T-shirt instead of my sweatshirt and my gaze snapped to his. "You changed my clothes."

"Yes, I did. Don't worry—I didn't take advantage of you. Just ask your dog, he watched the entire time. Your sweatshirt had blood and glass on it. I needed to take it off," he replied in a very calm, matter-of-fact voice.

"Garda didn't try to bite you, did he?" I asked.

"No, I'm pretty sure he figured out quickly that I wasn't trying to hurt you."

I nodded and grew pensive. "I don't know what to do," I said, peeking at Alex's face nervously.

"It's okay, I'll show you." He kissed my forehead. I closed my eyes and inhaled the scent that surrounded him. It calmed me in one way and brought on a strange excitement at the same time.

Alex walked to the other side of the room and reached down for something on the dresser. He returned and sat down on my side of the bed; pushing himself back, he propped himself against the pillows and headboard. I tracked him with my vision, afraid to move my body even a fraction of an inch. Once he was comfortable, he began unbuttoning his shirt. I watched his long, lean fingers manipulate each button through the hole, exposing another few inches of his chest each time. The view was intoxicating, and heat began to build inside of me. I had never been so turned on by a man taking off his shirt before. He pulled his shoulders from the sleeves, his eyes locked on mine, passion visible in his emerald irises. The silk shirt slipped off his fingers onto the floor with a soft sigh. His chest was perfection, muscular, his stomach flat, smooth, solid. My fingers itched to touch him.

Without a word, he reached for me, lifting me in his arms and pulling me against his chest as if I weighed nothing. My cheek nestled against his warm skin and I tensed when I found I could hear his heart beating. "Your heart beats."

He chuckled. "Yes—it beats, Kristin, and so does yours."

"Aren't vampires dead?" I lifted my face off his chest to see his expression.

"Our breed lives, our hearts beat. There is another breed that exists where the heart does not beat, and that is the one the horror stories are made from."

"Oh," was all I could say as I rested my head back on his warm chest. A drum was pounding inside my skull and sharp pains tore up and down my arm, but the sound of his steady heart under my ear calmed me. I snuggled harder against his chest, as if I wanted to burrow my way inside and he groaned. "I'm sorry—did I hurt you, Alex?" I tried to lift my head again, but he cradled the back and held it against his skin.

"No, you can't hurt me, Kristin, not physically." He paused for a few seconds. "You feel so good lying here on my chest, the feeling got intense for a moment." He wound his fingers into my short hair and rubbed my scalp softly.

"Oh." He had a way of taking my words away from me. What happened to the intelligent woman I normally was? She seemed to have disappeared when this handsome man arrived at my door. A few minutes later, Alex shifted me further up on his chest so that my head now rested on his shoulder, my lips an inch from his tantalizing neck.

I could see the vein in his throat, could feel the pulse of the blood running through his body. I could smell it, the coppery scent of his blood mixed with the scent of spices and coffee, and I felt a stirring deep inside my body. An ache began in my throat. How had I never noticed this before? Why was I now able to smell these things?

I pushed back so that I could lift my head. Our eyes met and I unconsciously licked my lips. Without thinking, I leaned forward and put my lips to his. The kiss was slow, gentle, coaxing. His smooth lips kissed me back in the same gentle manner. I parted my lips and swiped his bottom lip with my tongue. He shuddered and opened his mouth to join our tongues together.

The kiss grew deep, not frantic, but searching. A deep wanting spread through my body. I didn't know if it was sex that I craved, him, or his blood, but I knew I wanted him at that moment, more than I had wanted Julian earlier tonight. I felt a matching need coming from him. Alex drew back, keeping his eyes locked on mine, and reached over to the nightstand beside the bed. He watched me closely as he shifted the object in his other hand and pulled back the blade of my knife. There was a brief moment of panic, was he going to stab me? Was he going to slash my throat?

"I would never do anything to hurt you, trust me, Kristin." Those words settled me—calmed me. "This will make it easier for you to feed from me." He brought the tip of the blade to his throat and pushed it into his skin. My body trembled in a way it never had before.

Crimson blood beaded at the sight and then slowly ran down the column of his neck. I couldn't tear my eyes away. I licked my lips again, feeling an instinctive yearning take over my mind and body.

The sight of the blood flowing held me spellbound. I heard the blade click closed and felt it land on the bed behind me. I couldn't tear my gaze from his neck. He put his hand behind my head and gently pulled me forward. "Drink my love, drink," he said softly, as he pulled me closer to his neck.

The scent of his blood overpowered me, and I let my instinct guide me. I leaned into him and closed my lips over the small hole in his neck. The tip of my tongue touched his skin and with it a hot explosion of thirst, the taste so incredible, it matched nothing that had ever crossed my lips before. I sucked against his skin greedily. I tucked myself tighter against him, letting my tongue swirl around the warm fluid filling my mouth.

He groaned and I felt it as much as I heard it. His body shifted underneath mine as he pulled me to lie completely over him. Another burst of desire and I ground against him. The pain was gone now. With the first taste of his blood, the pain had begun to recede. Alex moaned deeply in his throat and pulled me tighter as his arms wrapped around my back. His hands glided over me, touching my back, my hips, my ass, but it wasn't enough. I needed him in more ways than I could have ever imagined.

His blood was consuming my soul and I wanted him to physically consume my body. I swallowed as fast as I could, craving more with each drop. His erection pushed against my thigh and I shifted to move it between my legs. I needed to feel him inside of me. God, I had never wanted someone as much as I wanted him at that moment. I whimpered against his throat when he held me still, not allowing me to rub against him.

I wrapped my arm around his neck and twisted him so that I was now under him, he chuckled, and the vibration enflamed me further. I was lost in the passion, the taste of him on my tongue. More, I needed more.

His hand slipped up my side to my chest and I pushed my breast into his palm, begging to be touched. He squeezed it gently before sliding his hand down toward my waistband—yes! Oh God! Please, yes. His hand dipped under the material and between my legs. I arched against his hand as his fingers fondled my soft wet folds. He stilled as I moaned against the hot skin of his neck.

"Alex," I said breathlessly as I pulled away from his neck. "Alex, make love to me."

His eyes were smoky, clouded with hot passion and need. He opened his mouth and I saw his canine teeth had extended long and sharp. I should have been scared, should have pulled back, but I wanted them. I wanted to feel them in my neck. This was how it felt to want to be possessed. He kissed me, licking the blood off my lips. Every nerve ending in my body more alive than it had ever been.

When he pulled back from the kiss, he withdrew his hand from my pants and pulled me tightly against him.

He inhaled deeply, holding it for a long moment.

"I want nothing more than to make love to you. Right here, right now. I want to make you mine, Kristin." He pushed off of me and moved back to a sitting position, licking his fingers and rubbing them over the cut in his neck that already seemed smaller. I watched in fascination as the skin healed instantly. Alex closed his eyes.

The distance he had put between us helped clear the haze from my mind. Jesus H. Christ, who the fuck was this wanton woman who had just thrown herself against a man that she didn't know and begged him to make love to her? I was mortified by my actions, but still wanted him more than air. "I hear a 'but' coming," I said quietly.

He looked down at me and sighed. "But I can't. I could never take you when you are in the throes of bloodlust. If it is me you want, you will need to come to me of your own accord, not while you are feeding from me, pulling the passion from my veins."

"But, Alex, I do want you. It doesn't have anything to do with the blood," I said, looking at him seriously.

He seemed to be thinking about something. Like he wanted to try out the words in his mind before he spoke them aloud. Still watching me carefully, he said softly, "But you want Julian, too." It was not said as a question. It was said as a fact and my face heated with embarrassment.

Julian...I did want Julian earlier, but not like I had desired Alex.

Could I possibly even want Julian after what I had just shared with Alex?

Yes…yes, it was possible that I could want him. It was possible I could want both of them. Oh, hell! I dropped back against the bed and draped my arm over my eyes to hide.

CHAPTER TWENTY-THREE

JULIAN

I roamed the house, not able to stop the feelings that consumed me. I tried to occupy myself with TV and magazines, but no matter what I did, I was restless.

I even fed again and took a long hot shower, but nothing could keep the haunting thoughts out of my mind. Nothing took away the memories of the night I had lost Calista, or the thoughts of what I would have to do now to keep her safe.

When I walked back downstairs to the main floor, I looked at my watch again. It was after midnight and Alex had not returned yet. I knew in the bottom of my dark soul that he was with Kristin. He was probably trying to find a way to convince her that he was actually the one she had loved.

I felt angry and sick, and I could do nothing but wait.

Alex ordered me to stay here, and I could not disobey. He was my boss, my master, and to defy him would be putting my life on the line. I could not protect Kristin if I was punished or destroyed.

Not long ago, I would have welcomed the idea of leaving this life behind in order to follow Calista into the afterworld, but now that I had found her again, I no longer wanted that. I wanted her.

I heard a car pull up the driveway and stop. My body hummed with tension, knowing that it would be Alex.

I leaned against the foyer wall, trying to be patient until he opened the door. My arms were crossed over my chest, to keep them from visibly shaking. I was afraid of what he would say. What had happened between them?

Alex stepped into the foyer and the crystal chandelier cast off sparkling light around the room and onto the dark hardwood floor.

I was like a snake coiled to strike as I took in his appearance, his suit jacket thrown over his shoulder, his blue dress shirt unbuttoned more than he normally wore it. Wrinkles embedded into the material as if it had been tossed aside and abandoned in the heat of passion. My eyes flared, anger rising in me. I inhaled sharply and caught the smell I feared I would.

Her blood…his blood…the two together.

Alex heard my gasp and stopped just inside the door, alert and ready for what he knew was coming.

"Don't, Julian. It's not what you think," he said, watching me carefully.

"Not what I think? Fuck you, Alex! This was the perfect way to get back at me, and you know it," I sneered through clenched teeth, my arms still crossed, and hands clenched so tightly they ached.

He stepped deeper into the room and her scent ran off him like water in a shower, filling the air around me, invading my senses—and I could not hold back any longer.

I threw myself off the wall at Alex. He anticipated the move and shifted quickly to the side, throwing his suit jacket out of the way as he barely avoided me crashing into him. He got behind me and pushed me forward, crushing me between his body and the stone wall.

Alexander was older, bigger, and stronger than me. I could fight him, but I knew I could not win against him if he was prepared to fight, which he was. "Jules, stop!" he shouted. His arm pushed against the back of my neck, forcing my face up against the cold stone. "Stop and I will explain."

"Explain what, Alex? Explain that you took her to bed and mated with her? That you took her blood, and let her feed from you and now she is yours? You don't have to tell me that—I can smell her blood; I can still see where she fed from you."

"If you know so much, Julian, then you will know I did not mate with her! Open your senses and you will see I did not mate with her and I did not feed from her! I did not make her my own! I would not do that!" he yelled in my ear, and then shoved off me, stepping back.

I closed my eyes and put my forehead against the cool wall, trying to bring my breathing back to normal. I reached out with my senses and could not feel the mating, could smell only a trace of her blood, not the strong scent that would be on him if he had fed from her. I turned to him. I wanted a real answer.

He stood in the middle of the foyer, both hands on his hips, head bent, staring at the floor. I could not see his eyes, but I could see the light pink scar on his neck and a blood stain on his shirt. The blood on his shirt was from someone else.

With a new vengeance, I slammed into him this time, catching him unprepared. I hit him so hard that our bodies flew across the hall and slammed against the wall on the other side. I put my forearm over his throat and pushed him hard against the surface, slamming his head back against the unforgiving stone. He closed his eyes and flinched momentarily.

"Who hurt her? What happened to her? I can smell her blood on you, and you fed her—I can see that now! If you didn't mate with her, then you wouldn't have had to feed her unless she was hurt. Did. You. Hurt. Her?" I bellowed in his face.

"Of course, I didn't hurt her. Calm the hell down, Julian. Let me go and I will explain."

After a few seconds, I took a deep breath and let him go, stepping back with my arms tensed at my sides, ready to go after him again. I knew that what I had just done, attacking him, would normally be a death sentence. I waited as meekly as I could.

He relaxed against the wall, twisting his neck around to loosen it up after I had held it so tightly. "Actually, she did it to herself," he said after a moment.

"Yeah, right! What did you tell her that made her want to hurt herself?" The anger still seethed in me.

Alex walked past me and into the living room of the house. He walked over to the fireplace and stood staring into the empty grate.

"Explain, Alex."

"I need a drink," Alex stated, and walked to the bar. "You want one?"

"No—explain, Alex, before I lose it again." I was so keyed up. Was she okay? Was she dead? Is that what Alex was going to tell me, that she was dead again after I had just found her?

He poured some whiskey into a crystal glass and threw the drink down his throat before pouring himself another one. He sank into one of the two high-backed leather wing chairs in front of the fireplace. "Sit, Jules," he said quietly.

My heart was hammering in my chest, and all I wanted to know was if she was all right. "Alex, is she…alive?" I could barely get the words out of my mouth.

"Julian, she is fine. Sit. She is fine." He took a sip from his glass.

I let the air out slowly and sank down with my elbows resting on my knees, staring at the floor in front of me.

"I was trying to explain to her what was going on. Telling her about us, about the Taylors, and why these things have been happening. I was telling her about Damon, and I told her what she really was." He spoke quietly. From the corner of my eye, I could see him staring straight ahead.

I turned to study him, to make sure that he was telling me the truth. "How did she take it?" How would she have felt? She hadn't known about us, or what she really was. She was raised a human. Most of us grew up knowing what we were and that one day we would be turned into a vampire to live out the rest of our long lives. What would it be like to live thirty-four years and not know what you really were?

It took him a while to answer and when he did, it wasn't what I expected.

"She laughed." He kind of snorted when he said it—half a laugh, half an expulsion of air.

"She laughed? Like she thought it was a joke?" I asked him, leaning back in my seat, the tension finally ebbing from my body.

"Yes, I think at first she laughed because she thought I was crazy. Then I think she laughed because she didn't know what else to do. When she finally stopped, I could feel a sense of hysteria building inside her." He took another sip of his drink. I waited for him to continue.

"I tried to calm her, but she fought me. She's strong Julian, wow. Stronger than I imagined her to be, but I was able to stop her. She calmed down for a moment and then she started to run from me. She tripped and fell over her own feet, and when she fell, she hit her head on the coffee table and put her arm through the glass top."

I stared at him, my mouth hanging open. "But she's okay?" I asked when I remembered how to talk.

"Yes. She was unconscious for a little while, long enough actually for me to stitch up her arm. That would be how I got her blood on my shirt." He looked directly at me when he said that, making a point about it.

I sighed and looked down at the floor again. I knew there was more. "Then what, Alex?"

It was his turn to sigh. "When she woke up, I told her she needed to feed in order to heal. So she did."

He said that like it was the end of the story, but I knew there was more. I knew what feeding entailed. I knew the feelings and passion that erupted in your body when someone took your vein. I didn't want to know the rest of the story, but I needed to hear it.

"And?" I asked hesitantly.

"And nothing. She fed; she fell asleep. She was healing quickly. I knew she would be all right, so I left."

"You didn't have sex with her, Alex? Did you try to mate with her? Did you want to?" I had to know the answers.

He threw back the rest of his whiskey, looked at me long and hard, and stood up, walking back to the bar to pour himself another one.

"No, I didn't sleep with her, Julian—and I didn't try, either. Did I want to make love to her? Hell, yes! Especially when she was clinging to me and asking me to, but I didn't." He turned around and glared at me. I felt the dig exactly as he intended me to feel it. Like a spike through my heart.

The thought of her clinging to him made my heart lurch, but I understood why he had fed her, and I understood what she would have felt. What I didn't understand was why Alex hadn't taken her.

"Why? Why didn't you then? If she was all over you, then why didn't you take her? It was your chance to get back at me. Why didn't you take it?" I stood as I spoke.

"Julian, I don't take women when they are in bloodlust. I take them because it is me that they want, not my blood flowing through them. It is also not time for Kristin to be turned. She needs to understand all this before she joins us." He shrugged his shoulders. "And besides, I didn't want to take away her choice."

"Her choice? Her choice of what?" A piece of me was angry, but I fought to keep it down.

"Her choice between you and me," he said simply. He downed his drink, set the glass down on the bar, and stalked out of the room. When he reached the threshold, he stopped. "You might think she is Calista—and yes, she looks and smells almost exactly like her—but she is not her. She is her own self, stronger and smarter than Calista ever was. She is Kristin and she is different from Calista. If you can't see the difference, then you are blind. She needs to make her own decision, and while I did not take her tonight, if she decides that it's me she wants"—he looked over his shoulder—"and not you—then I will take her without a second thought."

He walked out the room, leaving me staring at his back and pondering his words.

CHAPTER TWENTY-FOUR

KRISTIN

I woke around eight in the morning. I needed to get up and ready, as I was working an earlier shift for someone else today, but I was afraid to move. I feared the pain in my arm and head would return.

I lay still, replaying the night before. My whole life seemed to have been turned upside down in such a short time. Was it only the other day that I wondered what was missing in my life? Had it been just a few short days that I thought I belonged someplace else?

The answers seemed to have found me, or at least some of them did. I knew that they believed I was something different, someone else. Something that few people knew existed. Something that people feared. Had I really drank his blood? The thought of feeding freaked me out, but somehow it felt right at the same time. Would I need to feed on people to survive? I didn't know anything about being a vampire.

I reflected on feeding from Alex. I had felt light-headed and full of passion. I had wanted him, but he'd refused me, saying that he would not take me while I was in bloodlust. Is that what feeding from someone did to you? Would I feel the same fire and passion if I had fed from Julian?

Julian...fuck. How was I going to face Julian after what happened with Alex? Alex said I would have to make a choice between the two of them. How could I choose? Why did I even have to?

I had drifted off to sleep eventually, and Alex had whispered in my ear that everything would be all right and he would see me later. He had kissed my temple, pulled the covers up around me, and let himself out of the house.

My dreams had been silent last night, nothing but blissful sleep.

I needed to move and take inventory of my body and was pleasantly surprised that I felt no pain at all. I actually felt energized and more alive than I had in a long time. I ran a finger over the small pink scar on my arm. It was almost completely healed...okay, that part was pretty cool.

I laughed as I climbed out of bed and remembered how I ended up in bed in the first place. I had fallen into the coffee table. Shit. I went out to the living room intent on cleaning the mess only to find no signs of the events from the night before. No blood, no glass. My coffee table wasn't even in the room.

Alex had cleaned it? I tried to picture that tall, beautiful man cleaning the mess in dress slacks and his blue silk dress shirt. It was hard to imagine.

I let Garda outside and started the coffee pot. There was a strange feeling running through my veins and it seemed like the day was brighter, the colors bolder. I stood at the back door and was met by smells I had never truly discovered before. I slowly inhaled so that I could take it all in.

I could smell the grass, as if it had just been mowed, even though it had not. I could smell the bark of the trees as if I was resting my cheek on them. I thought I could even smell the sun. It was incredible.

I always knew I had a great sense of smell, eyesight, and hearing, but it was nothing compared to what I was picking up on now.

I quickly got dressed and headed to work. I had a lot to get done there, and I needed to find time to stop by the Taylors'. I wanted to speak with Mrs. Taylor tonight. I knew that she would be able to help me make sense of all of this.

When I got to work, I dressed in my uniform and put my gear into my truck. I felt as though I was walking on air, everything felt easier to do. I checked my voicemail and returned a couple of calls from residents who had questions about cases I was investigating for them.

There was one call I was putting off—the one to Detective Davis. I lucked out and he wasn't in. I left him a message and told him I would be on duty until ten.

When my voicemails and e-mails were taken care of, I decided I didn't want to hang out at the station and do any paperwork. I needed to move. I felt a constant need to move crawling under my skin, so I set off in my truck to do some patrol.

As I pulled into a neighborhood, I saw Cole, one of our day shift guys, driving through. We pulled up alongside each other and rolled down our windows.

"Hey, Kristin, been a while! You look good. Did you do something different with yourself?" He eyed me critically.

Cole enjoyed working day shift, as Mick and I enjoyed working night shift. It just kind of fit our personalities. I thought about the fact that it fit me even better now, or did it? Were vampires really night creatures?

"Nope, nothing different, Cole. What's going on? Anything happening around the township?" We talked about some incidents that had happened and he told me about what his wife and four-year-old were up to now. It was the normal banter between partners and eventually we split off to do roving patrols.

As the afternoon moved slowly along, I began to wonder if I would hear from Alex or Julian. Would either of them call me? What would I say if either of them did?

Part of me was dying to see them both, but the other part of me was afraid. I feared that I would have to make a choice, and I didn't know what it should be. How do you decide between two men whom you barely know? How much time would I have before I had to make the decision? Why a decision at all?

Around six, I called the Taylors. I wanted to see if Mrs. Taylor would be willing to speak to me.

On the second ring, she answered. "Hello, Mrs. Taylor?"

"Kristin, is that you?" She sounded happy.

"Yes, it's me," I answered nervously.

"Kristin, I think now is the time you should stop calling me Mrs. Taylor and start calling me Gina Marie." She laughed into the phone.

"Okay, Gina Marie, I can do that. Um…look, I was wondering if I might be to speak with you. I, um, have a few questions that I think you might be able to answer."

"Kristin, I have been waiting years to answer these questions. Yes! Of course, I will answer them." She sounded so excited.

"You were?" I was surprised by her response. "Gina Marie, did you know Calista?" I could barely ask that question, but I needed to hear the answer.

She spoke softly. "Yes, I knew Calista. She was my best friend and I have been patiently waiting the last thirty-five years for her to be that again. What time do you get off work?" she asked.

We were best friends? Why didn't she ever say anything?

"My shift ends at ten tonight," I said.

"Excellent! Stop by after your shift so we won't have to worry about being interrupted."

"Sounds good, I will see you then." It felt like a weight had been lifted from my shoulders as I hung up.

All of a sudden, I had so much more in my life. I now had friends I never realized I had, a life I didn't know anything about, a hunger for blood that completely freaked me out, and two men whom I seemed to have to choose between.

For a moment, I almost wished I was back driving aimlessly around wondering what was missing, because it was slightly over-whelming. The rest of my shift passed quickly with simple phone assignments and a couple of alarms. I didn't hear back from Detective Davis, and I was glad.

How could I tell him that the serial murderer was a vampire and that he was killing his own kind? I didn't truly understand it, and I was supposed to be one of them. Besides I didn't think that I was even allowed to tell anyone that vampires existed. Alex hadn't said anything about me not saying anything, but I had a feeling that it was an unwritten rule. So the longer my conversation was put off with Detective Davis, the better.

When my shift ended, I parked the truck in the garage bay and climbed into my Jeep. I had changed into a pair of jeans and a sweatshirt but was still wearing my work boots. It was easier to wear them than to carry another pair of shoes with me back and forth to work.

As I drove over to the Taylors' house, I wondered again if I would see Alex and Julian there. I had not heard from either one of them tonight and wondered why.

I pulled up to the Taylors' house and saw it was nicely lit up. I guess I'd never really paid attention to the fact that their house was lit up late into the night while all of the houses around it were dark and quiet. I guess that was something I should start paying attention to. How many other vampires lived in and around Fawn Hollow?

There was a silver BMW in the driveway that I knew didn't belong there. I couldn't see the license plate, not that it would have helped me. It wasn't as if I was in my patrol vehicle and could run the plate to see who the owner was.

With nervous anticipation, I headed up to the door. It opened before I reached it, and Gabe stood grinning down at me.

"Kristin! About time you got here. We've been waiting for you." He took my arm and pulled me into the foyer. "How was your night?" He had a happy-go-lucky kind of personality that made you like him immediately.

"It was good. Trivial actually, but good."

"Everyone is waiting in the kitchen, come on." He put his hand on my shoulder as he said it and led me down the hallway from the foyer into the brightly lit kitchen. It was a friendly gesture, but all at once, I had the feeling of being trapped.

If I tried to turn around and walk back out the door, would he let me?

I entered the kitchen and saw Gina Marie first. She was smiling like a fool. She rushed over and threw her arms around me, hugging me as if we had been friends forever. I guess in a way we had been, although I didn't remember it.

"Kristin! Thank God! You have no idea how long I have wanted to do this! Finally, I can share things with you like we used to. Oh my God, it's been *forever!*" She beamed, excitement oozing from her.

I laughed, embarrassed, but returned the hug the best that I could.

When she stepped back, Mr. Taylor came forward and put his hand on my shoulder. "Kristin, call me Brendon. You can't believe how happy I am that *she* can finally talk to you, too. For the last ten years, since she saw you again, you have no idea the countless times she has talked about you and worried about you." He smiled and squeezed my shoulder before he leaned down and kissed Gina Marie on the cheek.

I laughed nervously. Mr. Taylor, I mean Brendon, still intimidated me, even more so now that I knew what he was.

I had been so focused on Gina Marie and her husband that when I turned around, I finally noticed both Alex and Julian standing next to the kitchen table watching me; I took a step back.

I looked between the two of them. They were so different, yet so similar. One tall, with long brown hair and deep emerald green eyes, and the other shorter with trim, neatly cut brown hair and bright-blue eyes. Both of them had such chiseled features, and a paleness to their skins I had not noticed before. I swallowed as I looked at them, not sure what to say or if my voice would even work at all.

The currents that ran among the three of us were so thick, they couldn't have even been cut with a knife.

Thank God, Gina Marie took that second to break the tension. "Okay, guys. She's not a piece of meat, so stop staring at her like you are both starving."

Did I say she broke the tension? I almost groaned. Like a switch had been flipped, all the energy I felt during the day seemed to drain out of me and my knees felt weak. On the edge of my vision, darkness began to creep in, and I had the sudden realization that I was about to pass out.

Gabe put his arm around my waist, and two pairs of eyes glared.

Was that anger? Possessiveness? Fear? I didn't know, but both sets of eyes held the same look for just a second before Gabe spoke.

"Hey—chill, guys. She needs to sit down. She's about to pass out." He led me over to the table and pulled out a chair for me. I sat down and, in a matter of a second, a bottle of water appeared in front of me.

"Drink, Kristin. It will make you feel better," Gabe said quietly as he squatted next to me. His hand rested on my back, and while I could feel it against my skin, all my senses were picking up the two other men who were standing to my left next to the table.

The feeling eventually ebbed away, and I shook my head. "Thanks, Gabe," I said quietly.

I heard feet move to the side of me and the sound of a chair being pulled back. Someone sat down and I caught a whiff of spices and coffee settling around me. Alex.

I lifted my chin and smiled shyly. He winked and returned the shy smile with one of his own. I never pictured Alex as being shy.

"How are you feeling, Kristin?"

For a moment I thought he would reach out to me, but he held his hand back. "I'm okay now." I lifted my chin higher, trying to convey that fact, although I was far from okay.

"How is your head feeling? Let me see your arm." He reached across the corner of the table toward me, and I felt tension fly across the room again.

I scanned the room nervously. Julian seemed ready to jump at Alex. Gina Marie and her husband were watching as if they had no idea what was about to happen, and Gabe seemed like he was prepared to jump in to break up a fight if he had to.

A bubble of laughter erupted from my mouth before I could say anything. "Um—relax, everyone." I shifted my eyes around the room again, waiting until everyone appeared to have done what I asked.

I lifted my arm to the table and Alex pulled up the sleeve of my sweatshirt. The light pink scar was just barely visible now on the inside of my arm. Again, I was thinking the power of vampire blood was pretty freaking awesome.

"My head feels fine, and my arm, too. Thank you for last night,

Alex." I knew everyone in the room, especially Julian, was hanging on my every word.

"You're welcome." The look he gave me conveyed more feeling than any words ever could.

I pulled my arm back from his light touch. When I looked up again, everyone was still watching me.

"Okay, everyone can just stop staring at me like I'm a time bomb. I'm not going to detonate tonight." I said the words hoping to calm everyone, but suddenly I needed to move around, and I stood quickly.

The five other people in the room went into alert mode with my movement. Gabe, being the closest to me, put his hands on my shoulders—I wasn't sure why, but I suddenly began to feel calmer. The fight or flight receded from my mind.

"You know, this would all be a lot easier if everyone would just stop staring at me, waiting for something to happen." I glanced around the room and made sure to look a bit longer at Julian and Alex, hoping they would understand that I was talking more to them than anyone else.

"Hey, Master Alexander, Julian—why don't you guys head out and give Kristin some time to talk to Gina Marie and Brendon? I think she could use a few minutes to let all this sink in." Gabe squeezed my shoulders gently, and at that moment, I knew Gabe and I were going to be great friends. He was acting like a big brother right now, and I'd never had anyone act like that. It was nice.

Gina Marie and Brendon agreed with Gabe and waited for a reaction from Julian and Alex.

Julian nodded. I had not heard him speak a word the whole time I was here.

Alex approached and took my hand. A tingle ran up my arm and I started to take a step toward him, but Gabe held me fast, for which I was eternally grateful.

Alex flicked a look at Gabe before giving me his attention again. "I think that is a good idea." His eyes were a brighter green tonight. "You visit with Gina Marie and Brendon. You can ask them whatever you need to ask them. They will tell you all that you need to know."

He looked at Gina Marie with a pointed look. A silent conversation seemed to go back and forth, and then she nodded.

"I will talk to you soon." Alex kissed my cheek, his scent made me feel dizzy and my knees began to shake again. He stopped at the doorway and looked at Julian. "Jules, are you coming?" It was more of a command than a question; I had already figured out his authoritative voice.

Julian narrowed his eyes at Alex and took a step closer to the door. He stopped beside me and gazed into my eyes. It was all I could do to hold myself upright as I stared back, and my knees shook harder. Gabe squeezed my shoulders gently and I felt peaceful again.

Julian didn't say anything out loud, but when I heard a voice in my head, I knew it was him and tried not to react. *I'm sorry about last night. When you are ready to talk, we need to.* He didn't say anything else and left the room.

I stared at his back, fascinated that he could communicate with me without opening his mouth. Damn! Could he read my thoughts, too?

He must have looked up at Alex as he walked toward him, because Alex had a heated look as Julian neared.

I heard Julian speak out loud as he passed Alex, a single word meant for me, I knew. "Yes."

Alex gave me one last long look before he followed Julian. His stiff shoulders told me he was not happy about the silent exchange that Julian and I had shared.

When I heard the front door close, I stepped away from Gabe and dropped down in a chair.

Putting my face in my hands, I groaned, "Holy, hell!"

CHAPTER TWENTY-FIVE

ALEXANDER

*S*eeing Kristin again tonight after having felt her emotions all day was like finally unwrapping a present. A present that I had asked for and knew I was going to get but had to wait for Christmas morning to actually open.

We had all been sitting around Gina Marie's kitchen talking about Damon and how we were going to find him, when we heard her Jeep pull up in the driveway. Both Julian and I tensed immediately.

"I'll let her in—you guys just stay here and try not to freak her out, okay?" Gabe might have been young, but he was smarter than he appeared.

Gina Marie grinned like a kid in a candy store, ready to run down the hallway to greet Kristin the minute she walked in. We heard Gabe open the door, and when her voice rang out from the hall, both Julian and I stood immediately.

Gina Marie studied us with half-closed eyes, telling us without words to behave. I felt the tension and excitement wafting off of Julian—the same emotions I was feeling, too.

All of us felt the apprehension in the room, including Kristin.

When I approached her, I felt Julian twitch behind me. I sent him a silent message, *"Don't even think about it, Jules. You will not make a scene here. If you do, there will be consequences. We might love the same woman, but I am the Master."*

Julian growled into my mind. Gabe watched us closely. He was an emotions person, too. He could not only feel them, he could control them. Knowing that is the only reason I allowed him to put his hands on Kristin. I knew that he was trying to keep her calm and in control. Being this close to Kristin, I could feel my blood rushing through her veins. It called out to me and I had to fight not to touch her. I glanced at Gabe. *"Stop me if I touch her and it becomes too much,"* I said silently to him.

"I will, sir."

Gabe was right that we needed to give her time. All of them, except Julian, were sending me silent messages to give her that space. As hard as I tried to leave without touching her, I couldn't. I needed to feel the connection, if just briefly. The moment I took her hand, my blood called out to her and she moved to me. Gabe stopped her. I glared at him.

"You told me to stop you, sir." I couldn't be angry at him for doing what I asked.

I turned to Gina Marie before I left. *"You tell her what she needs to know, but under no circumstances do you tell her about me. Understand?"*

"Yes, sir."

Kristin's eyes were light blue now, and as if possessed by something else, I leaned down to kiss her cheek. Her soft scent of butter and sugar drifted around me gently. I let go of her hand with regret and turned to leave.

Julian had not moved as of yet. "Jules, are you coming?" I was not asking; I was telling him.

"Another order, Alex?" He asked me silently, as he glared at me.

I had no idea that Kristin had advanced enough to hear voices. Knowing that Julian had figured it out already pissed me off.

My jaw clenched as Julian approached me. *"I will fight you for her no matter what you order me to do,"* he said as he walked past me.

Julian and I were silent as we walked to my BMW.

I peered at Julian while I was driving. He was anxious and waiting for me to speak.

"Julian, I don't want to fight with you over her. I only want her to be safe and happy."

"And you think I can't keep her safe?" he tossed back.

I waited a moment before I answered him. "No, that's not it at all. It wasn't your fault that Calista was killed."

"Yeah, right. You can say that all you want, but I know you blame me for everything that happened, from the night I mated with her until the night she died. You hate me for everything that happened." His voice calmed, but the frustration he held was not for me, it was for himself.

"I don't hate you Julian. I never did," I said quietly.

He scrutinized me for a long time. "You did, too."

"No, that's where you are wrong. I was jealous. I was angry because I waited too long, but I was not angry with you, not really. I was furious with myself."

"But I didn't keep her safe." He looked out the passenger window.

"Julian, I blame myself for not keeping her safe. If I hadn't been such a fool about mating with her back then, she would have been mine and she would have been protected by all that I had."

He considered that for a moment. "You can't blame yourself, Alex. Just like I know I shouldn't blame myself for what happened. It's hard though. If it weren't for me, Damon wouldn't exist."

"And if it wasn't Damon, it would have been something else. That's not the point. We both made mistakes. Because I wasn't ready to commit to her—" What I was about to say stung, but it was far past time to clear the air with Julian. "I pushed her to you."

He glanced my way but turned away without saying anything.

"Jules, do you know what pissed me off the most about the whole thing?" I asked after a short silence. I wasn't sure I should say this, but part of me really wanted to get it off my chest.

He waited for me to speak.

"If you had just had sex with her, I wouldn't have cared. I mean—I would have. I would have been pissed, but I would have forgiven both of you. I would have still loved her, still wanted her…but you had to drink her blood and allow her to drink yours." My hands tightened on the steering wheel as I spoke, and I had to remind myself to loosen up before I damaged it. Julian didn't speak for a while.

"I never expected that to happen. It wasn't planned, Alex. I won't deny that I didn't think about it, but I never expected it to happen, not like that, and not that quickly. The chemistry between us was just too much and we both got caught up in it." Julian shook his head before he continued. "I used to wonder if I had done the right thing. Sometimes, I used to think that she would have been happier with you, like she would have gotten more out of her life. As much as I loved her and wanted her to be happy, I sometimes had the feeling that she wasn't, not entirely. Even though she said she was."

I was shocked by his admission. I didn't know how to respond.

As we pulled into the driveway, I turned to Julian and spoke. "Jules, we both need to allow Kristin to figure this out on her own. I promise you that until she has the time to decide what she wants; I will not feed from her. She already has my blood in her, and you have my word that I will not mate with her without her choosing me. I would like to request that you do the same and not share blood with her until she makes her choice."

"Why did you give her blood in the first place, Alex?" he asked. "Her wounds weren't that bad; she would have recovered quickly enough."

"Yeah, she could have healed on her own, but I did it so I would be able to pick up on her emotions. I want to know if she is in trouble or if she is afraid. It was the easiest way to be able to protect her without hovering over her."

"I guess I understand that." We climbed out and he looked at me over the top of the car. "Fine, we have a deal. I won't mate with her before she makes her choice. I think that is a good decision."

I was glad that we seemed to have buried the hatchet for the time being. Who knew what would happen after Kristin finally made her choice.

I scanned the area, "I think one of us should go back to Gina

Marie's house and watch her. I have a bad feeling tonight and I think it would be smart to keep an eye on her when she leaves to head home," I stated.

"Good idea, Alex. Do you want me to head over, or did you want to?" He was trying to remain calm. He knew that even though we were talking now, there was still a lot of animosity between us.

"Why don't you go now? I have several phone calls I need to make, and I have to check in with the office. Call me if anything happens. I'll take over for you in a few hours." As I walked into the house, I hoped that he would stay true to his word and not share blood with her. I wanted Kristin to know her options. I didn't like knowing that Julian thought she hadn't been happy all those years ago. I wanted to make sure that she was happy this time. Whether it was with him or me, I wanted her to be happy.

CHAPTER TWENTY-SIX

KRISTIN

*A*fter Julian and Alex walked out the door, I sat for a long time with my head in my hands, trying to think. Could everyone hear what I was thinking? Could everyone speak without words?

It took a while to realize Gina Marie sat beside me. My thoughts had been so loud and wild, I forgot others were around. Then I noticed that we were alone. "Where did Gabe and Brendon go?"

"They went downstairs to the man cave to watch TV. They figured we could use some girl time." Her long legs were crossed, and her hands were resting in her lap, relaxed. I wish I could feel that relaxed.

She laughed and said, "You will in time."

"Can all of you do that?" I asked, looking at her from behind guarded eyes.

"What? Hear your thoughts? Talk to people using our minds?" When I nodded, she continued. "Yes. As a half-breed—and that is what you are considered until you finish your transition—you are limited in being able to communicate with others. After you finish, you can communicate with almost all vampires and half-breeds. Some humans, too, but we are careful about that."

When I didn't say anything, she continued. "You were never taught how to hide it. There are ways, and I will teach you. It's kind of like putting up a wall around your mind. You can let it down for everyone or for just one person at a time." She cleared her throat. "Vampires are very good about locking thoughts down. We can communicate easily with each other by directing our thoughts to the other person. That person needs to be willing to accept them though, in order for them to be heard."

"So while everyone was here, all of you could hear what was going on inside my head?" I felt kind of violated by that thought.

"Yes, you project loudly." She laughed before continuing. "Even if we hadn't heard your thoughts, your emotions were so obvious that we would have known basically what you were thinking anyway, just by the feel of them."

"You feel my emotions, too?" Okay, now I really felt violated.

She laughed. I'm not sure if it was because of the question, or the violated comment I made to myself. I really needed to learn to put up that wall, and quick.

"We can feel emotions, especially Alex and Gabe. Alex is a master at feeling emotions from others, and now that you carry his blood in you, he knows every emotion you feel, even if you try to hide it." She watched me closely to see how I took that bit of information.

I shook my head—I didn't feel like talking about his blood running through my veins. "Can you only do this stuff when you are directly around someone? Like in the same room, or can it be anywhere?"

"No, distance is a big part. If you are not linked to someone by blood, you need to be close to them physically, like in the same area. But if you are linked by blood, your distance can be much greater. Brendon and I can communicate from a long distance, but we have to know the other is trying to communicate. It is also easier the older you are."

I listened intently as she continued. "If I want to talk to Gabe, I need to be pretty close to him, like within eyesight—a room or two away is about as far as we can manage. Although, like I said, Alex is very good at feeling emotions, and since you have his blood, he knows what you are feeling no matter where you are."

She smiled as I rolled my eyes and thought, *Oh, great!*

"Gina Marie, why does everyone think I'm Calista?" I was finally relaxing and decided now was the time to really start finding out some answers.

"Calista was an incredible vampire. She was so strong-willed and loved life. She lived her half-breed life to its fullest and sometimes I wonder if she would've been happier if she hadn't mated." She seemed thoughtful.

"She wasn't happy? Wasn't she in love with Julian or Alex?" I was kind of surprised at what she just said.

"No, she loved Julian. Worshipped him, almost. I think that because she felt so much for him, she lost a piece of herself. She just didn't seem as carefree and outgoing as she had been before they mated. Maybe that was from the guilt of mating with Julian without telling Alex. She did love him too." She shrugged her shoulders.

I was confused about that part of the story, but there were other things I needed to understand first. "Okay, but that still doesn't tell me why everyone thinks I am her." At least, I didn't think her answer had explained that.

She leaned forward, smiling, looking almost excited. "You look almost identical to her. You talk like her, you even smell like her." She laughed as I sat back a little bit in my chair, looking at her wide-eyed.

"Smell like her? What did she smell like? What do I smell like?" I sniffed the air, but I could pick up only the fresh sweet plum smell that seemed to be coming from her.

She laughed again. "You smell like sugar and butter mixed together. When you were with Julian, the two of you smelled like cinnamon buns fresh out of the oven. If you were with Alex, you mixed just as nicely with his spices and coffee scent."

"So everyone smells the same thing I can? I noticed that was what they smelled like. I thought maybe it was their cologne or something."

"No, it is a unique scent to them. With you all in the same room, I was getting hungry and had the urge to bake." She laughed as she stood up. "You want a glass of wine?"

I nodded and scanned her kitchen as she went about pouring two glasses of red wine. Her kitchen was spotless, bright even though it was all black granite countertops and shiny stainless steel. It was warm and inviting and it felt good to be sitting here.

"Do you all eat food?" I had noticed when she opened her fridge to get the wine that there were the ordinary items inside.

"Yes, we eat food." She laughed. "I'm surprised that wasn't one of your first questions. It usually is."

"Yeah, well, don't you have to drink blood? Do you kill people?" I asked this quietly because I was afraid of the answer.

"Yes, we drink blood, but we don't kill people. I mean, we easily can, but we don't. Most blood is purchased through a donation service. Of course, we share blood with our mates too, but mostly it is the donated blood that keeps us going. We don't physically have to eat food, but we enjoy it and it doesn't hurt us, so we do."

I contemplated what she said and then changed the subject back to wanting to know why they still thought I was Calista. I knew if Gina Marie was following my thoughts, she would understand when I started talking about something else.

"Okay—so everyone has a doppelganger, we all know that. Maybe I just look like her, so I'm a freak of science. I still don't understand why you all think I could be her." I took a sip of the wine, enjoying the fruity flavor as I swallowed.

"It's more than how you walk and talk. It's your personality, the way you view life, and move through it. You want to take control of everything, and she always did, too. Back in the '60s and '70s it was a strange thing for a woman to be bold and controlling." She laughed, as if she was recalling a distant memory.

"I have watched you over the years, and every time I saw you, it was like I was looking at Calista right there next to me. Tell me, Kristin, do you ever dream about things that seem so real, and you don't know why?"

I thought for a second. "Yeah, for a long time I've had unusual dreams, and recently they have been getting more detailed, and more frequent."

"What is one of the things that you dream about?" she asked curiously.

"Well, I have dreamed about a midnight-blue Mustang, and..." I stopped and looked up at her, feeling the heat on my face rise. She tried to hide the grin; it didn't work; she had heard the rest of the thought in my head.

"That isn't a dream, Kristin. That was real—it happened, and it happened with Julian. That was the night you mated with him. It was a night for strong emotions, and it stuck inside your soul. What else do you dream about?"

My mouth hung open. "It was real?" Suddenly, when she said that, it was as if she confirmed it, like she brought back the true memory. I could almost recall every detail of that moment. She stayed quiet, allowing me to run through the memory quickly.

"Kristin, your e-mail address...Nitewolf1369..." She looked at me to make sure I was listening and wasn't still stuck in the memory.

"Yeah, what about it?" I didn't know where this was going.

"That was actually your home address...1369 Nitewolf Court." She spoke softly, watching me carefully.

"You're kidding me. Are you serious?" Was I really remembering this stuff? Had I retained some of my past life?

She nodded.

"Damn...okay, what I really don't understand is—Calista died, right? How did she die? And how is it possible that I came back to life again?" These were the tough questions.

"Yes, you were killed. Damon killed you." She stopped to see if I had known this, but Alex had already told me that part. I just didn't know how.

"Damon ripped your throat out like he did to Dawn, but he didn't stake you in the heart, also like my daughter. If Julian hadn't been there, and tried to stop him, Damon would have staked you and your soul would have been gone for good." She leaned on the table, looking into her wine glass.

"So that's why Brendon asked if Dawn had a hole over her heart. He wanted to know if her soul had survived." Things were starting to click now.

"Yes, exactly! When you said there was no hole, I knew that there would one day be a chance that I would see her again, and even if I never do, I know that she will have another chance at life."

"That explains why you weren't emotional." I smiled weakly.

"Well, vampires aren't really all that emotional anyway. You kind of lose some of that as you get older." She took a sip of her wine. "Although, we are extremely passionate."

I snorted. "Yeah, I kinda figured that out." I swirled my wine around the glass. "How old are you?"

"I was thirty-four when I was turned, and that was forty-one years ago, so I'm basically seventy-five." She waited for a reaction.

I stopped swirling the glass and stared at her. "Seventy-five? Well...damn, you look freaking awesome for your age." We both laughed at that.

"Julian is over a hundred give or take a decade or two. Brendon is a hundred and fifty-six. Alexander, I think, is around two hundred and seventy-five, give or take another ten or twenty years."

"Are you kidding me? Holy crap! I can't even imagine being alive that long." I was stunned. "How long do you live?" I looked up at her when I asked.

"Forever...unless you are killed, you can live forever. I think the oldest vampire I know is well over a thousand years old." She smiled.

My jaw dropped open. "Seriously?"

"Kristin, there is something else you need to know about the night that Calista died." She seemed hesitant to tell me, and I could tell she didn't want to look me in the eye.

"What is it, Gina Marie?"

"Damon also killed someone else when he killed you." She watched me closely.

So? From what I was gathering, Damon had killed a lot of people. Why would this person be so difficult to talk about? I waited for her to continue.

"Damon killed Anastasia." When I didn't react, she continued. "Anastasia was your daughter." It was said very quietly, but it sounded loud in my head as it echoed through my mind.

A daughter? I'd had a daughter, and Damon had killed her? "How old was she?" I asked without looking at her.

"She was five, and she looked exactly like you and even had your crazy strong personality." She laughed quietly.

"Was her heart pierced?" I could barely ask the question.

"No—no, it wasn't. Damon didn't have the chance to do that before he went after you." She leaned forward as she spoke and rubbed her hand down my arm.

"So someplace out there, she exists? Right?" I asked hopefully.

"We believe so. We have always believed that if your body is killed and your soul is not destroyed you will come back again. Although, no one has ever come back quite exactly as you have, as far as we know." She sounded in awe of that.

So there was a chance that out there somewhere was a daughter of mine. Would I ever meet her? Would I ever know who she was? For all I knew, she could live right here and be my age. It was too much to think about right now, so I shoved it aside.

"I need to change the subject, Gina Marie. I'm not ready to think more on that right now." I stopped for a second and took a deep breath. "So, what about the sun? Can you go out in the sun?" God, the thought of never seeing the sun again made me tense.

"The younger you are, the more you can handle. Most vampires can handle dusk and dawn light pretty easily. I don't know any that can be out long after about eight in the morning, and it depends on the season. Since the sun is stronger in the summer, we can't go out under it as long. The winter is different since the sun is farther away." She was very matter of fact and seemed happy that we had moved on from the Anastasia conversation. "Half-breeds can handle the sun well, until they start the transition."

"Okay, so I'm fine right now and I'll at least be able to see my sunrises and sunsets then." I would have been very sad if I wasn't going to be able to ever watch the sun rise or fall again. Finally, I had to ask her. "Gina Marie, what was Alex to me?"

She pondered my questions. "You loved Alex, too."

I blew out a heavy breath and swirled the liquid in my glass.

STACY EATON

"Everyone thought that the two of you would be mated. Whenever Alex was in town, the two of you were constantly together. He was a ladies' man back then, and while he fathered other children, he had never mated with anyone."

She emptied her wine glass and continued. "I think you were tired of waiting and wanted to get back at Alex for making you wait so long to be taken. You wanted him to put you through the transition, you wanted to mate with him and be with him more than anything. I know you didn't plan on mating with Julian that night. I think it was just supposed to have been a one-night stand kind of thing, but the chemistry between you and Julian was so freaking strong. I don't know how Alex didn't notice it the night you and Julian met."

"Did Alex ever take a mate?" I held my breath, afraid of what the answer would be, and more afraid of how I would feel when I heard it.

"No. After what happened with you and Julian, he never took a mate. It is my understanding that he hasn't even been with another woman since then." She stopped talking and looked down. "Alex didn't want me to tell you these things."

"Is that the silent conversation you two had right before he left?"

"Yes. He basically told me to keep my mouth shut, but I'm not really good about that." She laughed.

"Will you get in trouble?" I didn't want her to get in trouble because I wanted answers.

"Alexander might be our Master, the leader of our breed, but you and I"—she pointed between the two of us—"we are best friends, and if you can't share the juicy stuff with a best friend, who can you share it with?"

She swiped a hand through the air as she laughed. "Don't worry about Alex, he doesn't scare me. Don't get me wrong, I would never do something to hurt him, or another vampire, but it's not fair for you not to know the whole story."

I felt so tired, and I looked at my watch to see that it was after one in the morning. I yawned as if just seeing the watch reminded me that I should be sleeping.

"Why don't you stay here tonight and get some sleep?"

"Thanks, but I need to get home. I have a dog who is probably already sitting with his legs crossed waiting for me to get there."

"Okay—then I'll tell Gabe to follow you home. Make sure you get there safely." She stood up as if she was going to go get him.

"No, I'll be fine. Gina Marie, I work night shifts by myself all the time and I'm safe. I know how to take care of myself."

"You know how to take care of yourself with humans, but Damon is out there, and if he knew who you were, he would try to kill you again. We just found you. We don't want to lose you." She pulled me into her arms and hugged me tightly.

"I appreciate your concern. I really do, but I'll be okay." This time when she hugged me, I really hugged her back.

"Please, Kristin. If you don't want Gabe to follow you, then let me call Alex or Julian to make sure you get home safely."

"I refuse to be afraid of him. I can take care of myself; I promise." I smiled at her, and she released my arm.

A couple of minutes later, I was backing out of her driveway on my way home. I had so many thoughts running through my tired brain. Some were answers to questions that I had received; others were questions I had yet to ask. My mind was in overload and I just wanted to go to sleep.

CHAPTER TWENTY-SEVEN

JULIAN

I left Alex at the VMF house and drove the Mustang back to Gina Marie's. I would wait down the street for Kristin to leave and follow her home. I'd stay there until Alex relieved me later.

I was okay with the deal we had made. I thought that allowing Kristin to make the choice was a good idea.

Would Alex really have forgiven us if we'd just had sex that night? Yeah, he probably would have. We weren't like humans in that respect; having sex with someone else when you weren't mated was no big deal. Even the males of our race fathered children with other women after they were mated. Lust and need were natural in our world.

I thought back to earlier tonight when Kristin arrived at Gina Marie's. I'd wanted to go to her, just as Alex had. It had been obvious that she was leery of us both. I guess I shouldn't have been surprised, with all that she'd learned in the last twenty-four hours.

I had been angry that Alex had fed her. She would have healed just fine on her own, but I could understand why he did it, to be able to watch out for her. I couldn't fault him for that. I just wished I could have been the one to do that. It had made more sense that Alex had, though, since he could feel emotions so much stronger than I could, from much further away. Him being alive for over two hundred years made his ability much stronger than mine.

I knew that since she had taken his blood, her transition would be coming closer. Her body would already be starting to strengthen and change. She was probably already noticing that her senses were stronger, bolder than before. She would not move further into the change until she fed more. It wouldn't be until she mated and exchanged blood and body that she would begin to move over to our world. Her final step would be to bear a child. Once a child began to grow in her, one fathered by our kind, the transition would be complete.

I craved her, as I had so many years ago. The thought of exchanging blood with her and blending with her body, feeling her start to come alive under me, was a vision I wanted to live through again. Just thinking about the act made my body ache and my heart thud harder.

I had to stop thinking like this. I needed to concentrate on keeping her safe. I would not be able to deal with Damon killing her a second time. Would Alex be able to keep her safer? That thought hurt my heart, because I knew that he probably could. Would Alex make her happy? Happier than I could?

What would I do if she chose Alex instead of me? Would I be able to deal with that? Be able to deal with the loss of her again? I squeezed my eyes closed.

The sound of a car engine gained my attention, and I saw headlights on the road up ahead of me. Kristin's red Jeep turned onto the road in front of me, going the opposite direction. I started the car, staying at a good distance behind her. I didn't turn my lights on and hoped that I wouldn't run into one of her co-workers who caught me driving without headlights again. I could see just fine without them.

Kristin arrived home without any problems. I parked my car down the road and ran up through some trees near her house to make sure there were no problems there. I took a quick sniff around and didn't find any scents that seemed alarming.

Kristin got out of her Jeep, looking around cautiously. She sniffed the air and approached her house. She kept her eyes up and scanned around as she reached the door. After opening it, she let her dog out, walked back outside, and sat down on the front step.

"I know you're out there, Julian. I can smell you. Come out," she said toward the trees where I stood.

Wow, her senses were so damn impressive.

I hesitated only a second before I stepped out of the tree line. I stopped when I heard a warning growl come from her dog. The dog ran back and stood in front of her protectively.

"It's okay, Garda. He's okay." She ran a hand down the dog's back. The dog turned around and studied her before he sat down, keeping his sharp eyes on me as I approached.

"You are stronger than I thought you would be," I told her as I drew closer. I kept my distance to keep the dog calm.

"What do you mean?" She looked at me with her head tilted to the side.

God, she was so beautiful sitting there under the moonlight. "Your senses are strong. The fact that you were able to pick up my scent that far out is pretty impressive. I can't wait to see what happens when you complete your transition."

She laughed and looked down at the ground. "I've always had a pretty impressive sense of smell and hearing. I am kind of amazed myself at how much they changed after I drank from Alex."

I didn't think she meant to say that, and she immediately clammed up after she realized it.

"Kristin, it's okay. I understand why Alex fed you, but do you know why he really did it?" I asked her quietly.

She didn't meet my eyes but turned her head up to the stars. "To help me heal quicker."

"Yes, and for another reason, too." Her eyes jumped back to mine quickly.

"Why else?" she asked, guarded.

I turned away and looked up at the sky. I let out a long breath before I sat on the step next to her. Her dog watched me as I did but didn't seem upset by it.

She kept waiting. I felt her anxiety, but I stayed out of her head. Alex was right; I had been taking advantage of her not being able to hide her thoughts.

"Alex did it to keep an eye on you," I said without looking at her. I waited a second before I continued. "And to help start your transition."

The tension in her body was replaced by anger. Waves of it rolled off of her now like a tumultuous surf.

"I don't need someone to babysit me. I know how to protect myself. Gina Marie told me that he could feel all my emotions. I hope he knows that this anger I feel right now, is for him!" She stood abruptly and walked out into the yard, shoulders and back stiff as she looked up at the sky.

When she got up, her dog must have taken that as a sign that it was time to tend to his business; he jogged off toward the side of the house. I followed Kristin and stopped behind her, so tempted to pull her back against my chest.

"I'm sorry about all of this," she said quietly.

"Sorry? For what?" Why would she feel she needed to apologize?

"For not knowing who I am, for not knowing about my past. For not knowing if it is you or Alex whom I should choose. Or maybe neither of you." She grew quiet, her face still tilted up to the night sky. Her shoulders relaxed after a moment, and she twisted her neck around as if she was trying to work out the tightness.

"Kristin, there is no reason to apologize for any of that." Damn, I wanted to reach for her, to touch her, to hold her, but I was so damn afraid to do that. "Kristin, would you turn around and look at me, please?"

She inhaled deeply, let it out slowly, and then turned. I didn't think she knew I was as close behind her as I was, because when she turned around, we came face to face. Our eyes locked and we stared at one another.

"I want to pull you into my arms right now and kiss you. I want to hold you forever and protect you with my life." I was not sure how I got those words out, but I did. I didn't seem to have any control over them as they started to flow, and I stood very still, waiting to see what she would say.

"Right now, this very moment, that is exactly what I want, too," she said.

"But?" I knew there was one; I could tell by the tone of her voice.

"But…" She closed her eyes as if steeling herself for something and surprised me by taking a step closer.

"No but—I want you to do it." She started to lean into me, and I knew that I shouldn't be doing this, that I should have stepped back. I should have walked away and let her go inside to get some sleep, but I didn't.

As soon as she started to lean in, I wasted no time pulling her into my arms. I kissed her slow and softly at first, but it deepened and grew intense in seconds. Our bodies crushed against each other; our hands ran over whatever part of the other we could reach.

To hell with what Alex said, I was about to pick her up and carry her inside her house, drink her blood, allow her to feed from me, and take her every which way I could. I was no longer in control. Just like the first time I had been with her, when she was Calista, she was like a drug that I needed.

It didn't matter if it was right or wrong, I craved her. I wanted her, and I was going to take her. I knew she wanted me. Right now, she wanted me more than anything; she could feel the craving, too. She threw back her head, allowing me access to her neck.

My fangs lengthened as I ran my tongue down the column of her neck, feeling the pulse in her throat beat wildly as she knew what was coming.

Just as I was about to sink my fangs into her hot throat and drink deeply from her, she froze. Her entire body tensed, and she began to pull away, turning from me quickly. At the same time, I heard her dog growl off to the side of the house, and I caught the scent in the air.

The scent that made my blood run cold, the scent that I dreamed about in my nightmares, and the odor that had destroyed my life. The scent of Damon.

A growl exploded out of my body as I stepped around Kristin and pushed her behind me.

CHAPTER TWENTY-EIGHT

KRISTIN

For every question that was answered, two more seemed to pop into my head. They would have to wait until I had slept and could digest all that I had learned. My head felt as if it would explode with all this new knowledge.

I got home safely and pulled my Jeep up into the driveway. Before I stepped out, I did a search as I would have if I was at work, looking around outside my vehicle, looking for danger. Not seeing any, I opened my door and slowly stepped out. I used my wonderful new hearing to listen to what was around me.

I heard a small sound off to the left of the house, like a twig snapping under someone's weight. I hesitated and took a quick sniff of the air. Cinnamon…Julian was watching me. Probably making sure I got home safe. Fine, I was too tired to argue.

I let Garda out and figured I might as well get this conversation over with. "I know you're out there, Julian. I can smell you. Come out." I sat down on the step as I spoke.

Garda was surprised when Julian stepped out of the tree line where he had been standing. A deep growl filled his throat as he came back to stand in front of me. He was a good watchdog, and he protected me well.

"It's okay, Garda. He's okay." Garda seemed somewhat happy with that and sat on his haunches looking at me, and then watched Julian as he approached.

When Julian stopped in front of me, I couldn't help but think how beautiful his smile was. Combine that sexy smile with those eyes and it took my breath away. Gina Marie had already told me that Alex had given me blood to watch over me, so I wasn't sure why I got angry again when Julian mentioned it. The urge to move struck me and I stood and walked out into the yard, tilting my head back to stare up into the dark star-filled sky. The sky that reminded me of Julian's eyes.

I knew Julian was behind me, I could smell him, feel the heat of his body crossing the distance between us. "I'm sorry about all of this." I was sorry for more than he knew. It was time to test myself. I turned around and almost fell into his arms.

I was unable to move as I looked into his eyes. My God, those eyes of his just sucked me in.

"I want to pull you into my arms right now and kiss you. I want to hold you forever and protect you with my life," Julian said breathlessly.

"Right now, at this very moment, that is exactly what I want, too," I said in return, meaning it, but also knowing that I needed to know something.

"But?"

"But…" I stepped closer. He was like a magnet and I was being drawn to him, but was it more than what I felt with Alex? Was it different? Was it better, more fulfilling?

"No—but. I want you to do it." The kiss started out tender, but it was only a moment before we clung to each other, reaching for any part that we could touch. We held each other as closely as we could. The kiss so deep that I felt I was drowning in desire, unable to think, unable to process anything other than the feel of him.

How could you want someone so much? How could my body crave someone so deeply? Yet still want another at the same time? I wanted him, there was no doubt. I wanted to feel him on me, skin to skin. I wanted to feel his lips tasting me. It felt natural to pull my head back and give him access to my throat. The immediate instinct to allow him to drink from me was so strong that I could not deny it. I wanted to feel him pulling the blood from my vein, sucking the life from inside of me while I felt his weight holding me down, pinning me under him while he entered me over and over again. I wanted to drink from him, pull from his vein; I wanted to be his. Alex's face crossed my mind and it gave me enough pause to pull back the tiniest bit. I sucked air into my mouth and stilled.

Leather and death! The scent of leather and death filled my nose, burned into the taste buds on my tongue. I could smell him, taste him, but I couldn't move. Irrational fear paralyzed me. Garda began to growl, and then it was Julian's growl that filled my ears. It was a sound like nothing I had ever heard before, coming from deep within his chest. He roared as he pulled me behind him, searching for the source.

"You stay behind me until I tell you to run—then you run like hell into the house." He said this very clearly into my mind. I couldn't respond; I could barely move. Only my eyes were able to shift, and the air went in and out of my lungs in a stuttered cadence.

He had come for me. That was the reason he was here. Damon had come for me, again. He was going to finish the job this time. Drive a stake through my heart, destroy my soul. I searched with my eyes and ears, trying to locate him in the trees around my home. Garda stood at the side of the house, his heavy scruff up, growling slowly and sniffing the air, searching the same area I was.

"So your bitch came back," a sneering voice called out from behind us. The sound jarred me free and I spun at the same time as Julian, only now Julian was behind me. Standing twenty feet in front of me was a man dressed in a black leather trench coat. The tails of the coat flapped gently against his legs as he shifted back and forth on the balls of his feet. He was alert and intense and he reminded me of a drugged-out zombie.

His hair was long, dirty-blond, and hung around his face in dense waves. He had piercing blue eyes. Eyes that looked familiar. His face was full, almost round, but not heavy.

I realized, as I looked at him, that it was not the smell of him I feared, nor the sight of him standing there looking at me that scared me shitless. It was the sight of his fangs glistening in the moonlight, a set of long white fangs that extended far out of the top of his jaw.

I shuddered as I examined every inch of him, afraid to move.

"Damon, you will not touch her this time," Julian said viciously from behind me. He was slowly shifting to get beside me.

"So, Father—you think you can stop me this time? You didn't do so well protecting her the last time." He laughed.

Father? Are you kidding me? Julian was his father?

I could feel the fury rising over Julian. "You will not take her from me this time," he growled at Damon. Julian's fangs extended and I tried not to stare at them, instead I tried to focus on his body as he prepared to defend me. I thought about the fact that my life might possibly be about to end. What if this really was my fate? What if I was not meant to become a vampire? What if I was brought back to life just to lose it again?

Fear and anger raged through me. Nope, not gonna happen. I had faced plenty of homicidal maniacs in my job. I was not going to let this one kill me without a fight.

I reached behind me slowly, going for my off-duty Glock that was under my sweatshirt at the small of my back. I had no idea if the gun would hurt him or not. I didn't know how to kill a vampire, other than tearing their throat out or putting a stake through their heart. But maybe it would slow him down enough to give Julian the advantage.

"She is nothing. Since she is still a half-breed, she will die even quicker than she did the last time." Damon laughed and shuffled closer, shifting into a fighting stance.

I stepped backward. I knew that look. It was a look of true determination, of pure insanity. This was the first time that I felt utter panic at seeing it, though.

"It's your turn to die, Damon. I brought you into our world and you have done nothing but disgrace me!" Julian yelled.

"You brought me into a world that I didn't want to be in. I begged you to let me stay human. I didn't want any part of this life. It is a curse, NOT A LIFE!" Damon shouted back with a vengeance I had never heard before.

"You could have been such a great asset to us. You could have hunted beside me, instead of being the hunted," Julian said in a lower tone.

"I want nothing of this life. I have spent years killing off these stupid half-breeds and the children to kill off our race. They all deserve to die," he sneered.

I slowly backed away as they threw angry words back and forth at each other. They didn't seem to notice.

"Well, you will have nothing to do with this life anymore, because you are going to die. You are going to die, tonight." Julian's voice was steel as he spoke. He moved forward, crouched, ready to spring.

"Yes, I will die tonight, but not by your hand, and not before I kill that bitch. Not before I kill you. Then, I will die by my own hand," he yelled, and moved toward Julian.

"You will have to kill me to get to her!" They started circling each other.

It was then that I noticed Julian had a silver piece of metal in his left hand. A stake!

I held my gun down in front of me, ready to bring it up if Damon moved toward me. I knew that it wouldn't kill him, but it might stun him enough so that Julian could get to him before he got to me.

My hands shook. In all my years as a cop, I had never been in a true life or death situation. A situation where I might have to end someone's life to protect mine, or to protect someone else's.

Oh, God! *Where is Alex?* I thought quickly.

I had been moving backward and knew I was coming close to my driveway, coming close to where my Jeep was parked. Could I get inside my truck and get out of here?

Shit! The keys were inside the house; I'd dropped them there when I let Garda out.

Damon and Julian continued to circle each other. They were snarling as they grew closer to one another.

A noise from the bottom of the driveway caught everyone's attention. I glanced in the direction of the street at the same time that Julian did.

Alex. Alex was here. I almost sighed in relief, except that was when everything happened in quick succession.

While Julian and I were distracted by Alex's arrival, Damon used that to his advantage and spun toward me. I turned my head back from the driveway and saw him coming my way.

I raised my gun as he moved, pointing it center mass, going for his heart as I had been trained to do to kill humans. As I raised my gun and looked into his eyes, I saw pure hatred and rage on his face, but there was something else—sadness. Was there sadness for what he was doing? For all the hurt he had caused? I dismissed the thought and pulled the trigger.

He was only feet in front of me when my finger pulled back. The sound of the firing pin striking the primer exploded around me as I was hit with a staggering force from the side.

I was thrown back hard, by what, I did not know. It wasn't Julian, because I had seen Julian coming toward Damon from over his shoulder. It couldn't have been Alex; he wasn't out of his car yet.

I watched in slow motion as I started to go down. I felt my gun fly from my hand and sail into the air. I saw Julian close in on Damon. There was a look of surprise on Damon's face as he jerked back from the force of the 40-caliber bullet hitting his chest in the area of his heart.

I heard Alex scream my name and Julian growl like a wild animal.

I kept falling—I tried to stop myself, but I was so off balance and in shock that I couldn't turn myself enough to keep from hitting my Jeep. My head slammed into the front quarter panel and I felt my head bounce off of it, the sound almost as loud as the gun had been.

I couldn't help but close my eyes as I continued down. The pain in my head echoed as it ran down my neck and through my spine.

I managed to open my eyes as I hit the ground and saw the ends of a black leather duster flapping around legs that were almost to me.

NOOOOO! I screamed in my pounding head.

I couldn't keep my eyes open and as they slid closed, I thought, *I'm going to die.* I heard Garda barking ferociously from someplace near me as my mind went blank and I fell into myself once again.

CHAPTER TWENTY-NINE

ALEXANDER

I needed some time to unwind and think about everything that had happened in the last couple of days. I also needed to call the office and see what was happening back in New York.

I knew that Kristin was safe with Gina Marie. I could feel her emotions changing every few seconds. I didn't know what they were talking about, but I could tell that some of what they discussed made her angry and sad. Sometimes I felt a sense of humor coming from her and she would pass between being tense and relaxed throughout the hours they talked.

I also knew when she grew tired. Her emotions weren't coming as strong and I figured it was good that Julian was waiting for her. She had been through so much these last few days and her reflexes were probably slower than they normally would be.

Around one, Gina Marie shot me a text message. *She just left 4 home, hope U guys R watching her.*

I typed back to her quickly. *Julian is following home. We will be with her at all times.*

Good deal, she typed back.

How'd it go? I asked.

As good as could be expected. Lots of ???s, she quickly responded.

I loved text messaging. It was so much easier than having to talk to people. You got to the point and that was it, no babbling.

Good. You keep your promise? I typed back.

I had to wait a bit longer for a response than I should have. *As best I could...lol.*

Great. I sighed and typed her back, *Will discuss THAT later.*

She didn't reply so I put my phone on the desk, flipping up the screen on my laptop to check some e-mails.

My cellphone beeped again, and I picked it up and read, *She's home...will be in trees watching.*

K. Keep me posted, I typed back to Julian. I didn't expect a reply.

A few minutes later, I found myself reaching out for her, wondering what she was doing. She seemed to be having conflicted emotions.

I flipped the laptop screen back down and got up. There was no way I was going to be able to concentrate on this. I had a bad feeling, and I wanted to get to her.

Maybe I was nervous about Julian being with her. We had cut a deal not to force her choice; could I trust him? I wanted to, but could I really trust him?

I found myself running out the door and jumping into my BMW. I needed to get there. Something was wrong! I felt a menace in the air, a threat hanging heavy all around me. It wasn't coming from Julian or Kristin, but it was out there, and it was coming.

I raced down the driveway, turning onto the main road and putting my foot on the gas pedal. I should send Julian a message. Damn it! I hit the steering wheel. I forgot my phone sitting on the desk. The feeling of impending doom was rising around me and I felt tension coming from Kristin. I tried to focus on her to follow what was going on, trying to pick up on what she might be doing.

When I felt the flare of lust and excitement wash through her, I wanted to scream. Julian! Damn him! I knew I couldn't trust him—I should never have trusted him!

I had to get there in time. I had to keep him from mating with her.

Would I be on time? I was so angry that for a minute I didn't pick up on the quick change of emotion that burst from her.

Fear...

Why would she be afraid? She wouldn't be afraid of Julian, would she? No, she wouldn't be afraid of Julian, not like this. This fear was not just uncertainty; it was a true feeling of complete terror. Damon! Damon was the cause of that fear! I pushed harder on the gas, making turns at speeds that would normally be considered reckless.

As I took in her fear, I measured it. The fear kept intensifying. It was so strong that it was hard for me to move through it. I could not imagine what she was truly feeling if it was this strong for me, coming through the bond. I was almost there—I had to make it!

As I grew closer, I felt a determination mixed with her fear. I didn't understand that, but I embraced it. I wish that I could see through her eyes, could communicate with her verbally.

As I turned onto the driveway, I saw Julian and Damon crouched, circling each other. Kristin was walking backward with her gun drawn, putting distance between the fight that was about to take place.

My car must have caused just enough of a distraction that Damon got the upper hand, and I watched him turn toward Kristin. My car came to a screeching halt, and I threw open my door to get out before it was completely stopped. Kristin raised her gun and fired into Damon's chest. Damon flinched, but kept coming toward her. He would have grabbed her if the dog hadn't slammed into her and knocked her off her feet.

The dog hit her so hard that she flew sideways into her Jeep. I yelled her name as I got out of the car, panic taking over my senses.

I heard her head bounce off the metal of her car, saw the surprise and pain fill her features as she started to fall to the ground. Her eyes were closed as she fell, but I watched them flash open as she looked up to see Damon move down to her.

The dog started barking as Damon reached for her.

She closed her eyes again just before Julian grabbed Damon from behind. Julian flipped Damon around so fast that Damon was taken by surprise. Damon lost his balance, but I caught him just in time. Julian stood in front of us.

"You. Are. Not. My. Son," Julian said slowly in a voice I had never heard before and then he slammed the silver stake into Damon's heart.

Damon screamed and looked up at his father. "Finally!" was all he said before he fell to the ground and his existence ended with a rush of dust.

Julian watched the dust start to scatter. He didn't speak and he didn't move. He stood there watching the dust get picked up by the light breeze.

The dog had gone over to Kristin and had lain down next to her, resting his head on her shoulder, whimpering.

"You are one hell of a fighter there, boy." I squatted next to him and petted him before I reached for Kristin. I didn't want him to think I was going to hurt her. He looked at me, and then back to her.

"Yeah—I'm gonna take care of her, don't you worry." I reached over to check her pulse. She was breathing shallowly, and I wanted to see how badly she was hurt. I started to roll her over, when I heard Julian speak behind me.

"Is she all right?" He was afraid; I could feel it.

"Yeah, she's gonna be fine. Probably gonna have one hell of a headache when she wakes up, but she will heal quickly."

He nodded and started to walk away.

"Julian, where are you going?" I called after him.

"You will take care of her, right?"

"Of course, I will, Julian." I paused. "Are you okay?"

"I need some time. I need to be alone. Look, when she wakes up, just tell her…" He dropped his chin to his chest. "Well, just tell her I will talk to her later. I have to go." He walked down the driveway to where his car was parked.

I could only imagine what was going through his mind. He would be in complete turmoil, pain, and anger, and all the fear would be causing such an intense wave of emotions. I watched Julian disappear down the driveway and turned my attention back to Kristin. I pulled her into my arms; her head fell back, and I could see a lump rising on the side of it. I cradled her against my chest so that her head was supported better and carried her into the house.

As I crossed the threshold, I realized how close I had come to losing her again. My legs felt weak and almost gave out under me. I staggered for a second and leaned against the wall in the foyer. The dog rubbed up against me as if he was giving me enough strength to make my way back to her bedroom. I laid her on the bed carefully and thought about the fact that it had been only twenty-four hours since I had found her and almost lost her again.

I watched her for a few more moments before I went to the kitchen to find ice for her head.

After I climbed on the bed, I pulled her to me. Her head rested against my chest so that I could hold the ice against the bump. I listened carefully to her breathing, gently running my fingers over her face.

If the emotions I had felt coming from her earlier were any indication, she would choose Julian again. So this might be the last time I got to hold her, and I was going to take advantage of every second.

I lay on the bed with her against me, touching her softly, wishing it was me whom she would choose, but knowing it would not be.

I had lost her twice, or was it three times now? Once when she picked Julian, then again when she was killed, and now she would choose Julian again.

At least she will be alive, I thought. I might have lost her again, but at least she would be alive. Would that be enough?

CHAPTER THIRTY

KRISTIN

I started to hear things, and my mind began to sift up through the fog. I felt a sense of déjà vu as I opened my eyes and saw Alex holding me against his chest. He was watching me and gently running his fingertips over my face.

He was a lot more touchy-feely than I remembered him being. He had never been someone who liked to cuddle. He wasn't someone who did a lot of gentle touching.

Wait! How the hell would I know that?

Holy crap! The room spun. I remembered. I remembered Gina Marie, my heart clenched—Anastasia! I remembered her and Julian, Alex, and Damon—but more importantly, I remembered Calista! I sat up so fast that I shocked Alex and the surprised look on his face would have been comical if I had time to think about it.

"Alex, oh my God! Alex!" I sat with both hands flat on the bed, looking around wide-eyed, taking in everything and letting all the memories flood over me.

Damon…Damon had been bad, Damon was dead…was Damon dead now?

Alex sat on the bed watching a huge array of emotions run over

195

me. He obviously didn't know what he should do, and just sat there silently.

"Alex. Alex, where is Julian? I need to talk to Julian!" I started to climb off the bed and Alex grabbed me by the arm, trying to pull me back onto the bed.

"Kristin, you need to rest. You hit your head really hard when Dam—" He stopped himself, not sure if he should finish the sentence.

"When Damon tried to kill me again? Is that what you were going to say?" I watched his eyes grow wide.

"Is Damon dead?" I asked quietly.

"Yes."

"Alex, I need to see Julian. He needs me right now. Where is he? *Where is he?*" Alex had let go of my arm; his face stony. I grabbed on to his arms, almost shaking him, begging him to answer me.

"I don't know. He said he had to be alone, he needed to think," he answered quietly.

I looked around the room, and it dawned on me. The lake! The lake on Eagle Glen—he went to the lake to think, just like he used to do when we were together.

"I know where he is!" I jumped off the bed and turned to leave the room; after I took a few steps toward the door, I stopped and spun back around.

"Alex, wait. I need to speak with Julian, and then I owe you a huge explanation." His eyes looked so sad and it killed me to leave him like that, but Julian needed me. "Promise me you'll wait here until I get back."

I knew he had no clue as to what the rolling emotional tide was doing inside my body right now.

"Fine," he replied.

"Thank you, Alex." I looked deeply into his eyes and smiled. "I'll be back soon." And with that, I turned and ran down the hall, grabbed my car keys, and sprinted to the driveway.

I decided to take my Jeep, even though I really felt the need for speed and wanted to take my Challenger. Julian could hear so well that he would have heard the exhaust system from far away. I wanted whatever element of surprise I could get.

As I drove, a whirlwind of memories flew through my mind. They were mixing with the pounding of my head from where I had hit it, but the mixture told me I was alive!

The realization that I had been another person in another life was burning inside of me. How many other people were able to remember details and people from a past life? It was crazy, but all of a sudden, I knew everything, remembered every single moment.

I could recall meeting Gina Marie, and the first time I saw Alex and approached him, joking about his beer label. But more importantly, I remembered Julian and our life together with our daughter, my daughter. I squeezed both of my hands on the wheel. My heart was thudding dangerously hard in my chest as if it might explode at any moment.

As I pulled down the dirt road that led to the lake, my body came alive with nervousness. I saw the Mustang parked in the small dirt lot. I couldn't believe he still had the Mustang.

I cut the engine and jogged down a dirt path through a thick copse of trees, and when I found myself exiting them on the other side, I stopped and looked over the water.

There was a long fishing pier that ran from the shore out to about three hundred feet into the middle of the lake. During the day, it was full of fathers and sons trying to bond, and old retired men kicking back to kill another day.

Tonight, there was only one person on it, and he was standing way out at the end where it crossed into a small T-shape. He was leaning against the railing, looking up at the almost-full moon.

Julian.

I gathered my courage and walked slowly out onto the pier. He must have been so wrapped up in his thoughts that he didn't hear me approach. I'm not sure if he felt the vibration at his feet or if he caught my scent, but I saw him push off his forearms from where he was leaning and grip the railing with both hands. He seemed to be squeezing it hard and his shoulders and back were bunched tightly.

When I got within a few feet, I stopped and waited. His profile was so beautiful here in the moonlight. He looked so perfect, so handsome, and so very sad.

I wanted to reach out to him, to touch him, to hold him, but I knew I needed to say a few things first.

"Jules..." I started cautiously.

He seemed to tense even further with the sound of my voice. "What do you want, Kristin?" He didn't sound angry, he sounded sad.

I instinctively moved closer to him but stopped. I had to speak from where I stood. I needed to get this out.

"Jules, I remember." A small bubble of laughter came out of my mouth. I didn't know if it was because I did remember it all, or because I was so nervous. "I remember everything."

He looked down at the railing, sighed, and turned to me. "I'm sorry. Sorry you had to see what happened tonight."

"No, you don't understand. Julian, I remember everything. Yeah, I remember what happened tonight, but I remember the past. I remember you, and Anastasia, and Alex—and Damon, too. But more importantly, I remember being Calista." I said in a rush.

His eyes flashed and it took him a full second to fully understand. "You remember it all?"

"Yes, all of it! The night we met, the Mustang..." I chuckled. "Our life, our daughter, the night I died, and Damon. I remember it all." I shuffled toward him as I spoke.

He seemed to wilt a bit, his shoulders falling down. "I'm sorry you had to remember all of that."

"No! I'm not! Oh, Julian, you don't understand. I remember everything, and what's more important is that you can forgive yourself now. I know you have felt guilty ever since that night, thinking you didn't protect me. Thinking it was your fault. But it wasn't!"

"What are you talking about, Kristin?" He turned away from me and put his hands back on the railing, looking out over the water.

"Julian, I knew you had been working on finding Damon. Somehow, I found out that he was your son, and I thought that you wanted to find him to patch up some problem you had with him, like you wanted to mend fences with him. I didn't realize why you were trying to locate him, but I hoped that if I found him, then maybe it would help you. Help us." My voice lowered as I finished.

He looked at me over his shoulder, not speaking, waiting for me to continue.

"So many things were coming between us. So many things didn't seem to be right. We were growing so far apart, and I thought that if I could do something for you, then maybe it would help to bring us back together." I moved to stand next to him at the railing.

The cold metal under my fingers felt good and made it easier for me to focus. "I started looking for Damon myself. And I found him. I went to him."

A quick intake of breath came from Julian, and I saw him turn to study my profile.

"I went to him, Julian. I told him that I wanted him to come to you. He said yes, that he would, so I brought him back with me."

"You didn't!" He reached for my arm and I shifted out of reach before he could. It was impossible to think when he touched me. That had always been our problem.

"I walked right into his trap. I brought him home that night, and it played perfectly into his plans to kill us right in front of you."

He moved lightning fast and pulled me into his arms. Burying his face in my neck, I didn't know that he was crying until I felt a cool drop touch my skin. I held him, pulling him into me as much as I could.

"You can forgive yourself. It wasn't your fault. You don't have to live with the belief that Damon found us and came after us because of you. It was my fault. I put our lives in jeopardy." I stepped out of his arms, putting my hand up to his face and wiping the tears away that ran down his cheeks. "If anyone should feel guilty, it should be me."

"I have lived for thirty-five years believing that you both died because of me. That the case I was working against him was the reason you died." He reached up and wiped the tear that had just fallen from my eye.

"I know. I think that is why I came back. Why I came back to being as close to Calista as I could."

He looked at me with a puzzled look. "What do you mean?"

"I came back a stronger, smarter version of Calista to be able to figure out the truth and to make it right, with you, and with Alex." I sighed, looking down and stepping out of his arms completely.

"Does Alex know?" He let his arms fall to his sides.

"No. When I woke up and all the memories started flooding my mind, I knew I had to find you and tell you. I knew that you needed to forgive yourself. I know that it will take you a long time to deal with what happened with Damon, but now you can let Calista…" I hesitated before looking up at him again. "You can let me go. You can forgive yourself and move on."

I cradled his face with one hand. He leaned into it, closing his eyes for a moment.

"We made a mistake, didn't we?" he asked as he opened his eyes again.

"Yeah, I think we did. I think we got caught up in the chemistry. We've always had such incredible chemistry. And that would be the second thing I need to fix. I need to do what I should have done back then."

His smile was strained, and he took my face in his hands and looked deeply into my eyes. "I will always be a part of you. There will always be a part of me that loves you."

He placed a gentle butterfly kiss to my lips before he let me go.

"I know, no matter what, we will always share a part of each other. I love you, Julian, please don't ever forget that." I kissed him one more time, then turned and started walking down the pier toward the shore. My steps quickened, until I found myself running.

CHAPTER THIRTY-ONE

ALEXANDER

Kristin had come around amazingly quick. I feared what would happen now. Did her feelings for Julian outweigh the feelings we shared? Would she decide once and for all to take him as her mate? For so many years, I dreamed of Calista, dreamed of what I should have done, and of how it had all ended. Maybe I would be better stepping back and just giving them my blessing. Maybe we could all move forward with our lives from there. I had no doubt she would go to him anyway. Her lids fluttered and she looked at me with clear blue eyes for a few seconds before she jerked into a sitting position. In that moment, her emotions were flying like sparks off a firework. There were so many of them that I couldn't get a fix on what they were all about.

I was stunned that she had rushed off to Julian. In the back of my mind, I hoped she would choose me, but obviously she didn't. Why would she want me to stay? Just to tell me that she was going to be with him? Did I really need to hear that?

Why had I promised to stay? I was torturing myself waiting for her to return. She was only going to tell me what I already knew.

I waited for a little while and then decided I was a fool for doing so. I would head back to the VMF house and get my things packed. I left a note on her bed and got into my BMW.

I didn't want to feel the emotions coming from her. I didn't want to know the things she was thinking or feeling. I knew that over time, the blood bond I had with her would lessen and I would stop feeling so much of what was traveling through her, although it would never completely go away. At least, I would know she was alive and happy.

I shook my head, thinking it was just another punishment that I would live with for the rest of my life, knowing she was with another and that I had lost her all over again.

As I drove back to the VMF house, I tried hard not to feel her emotions, tried to block them out, but they were strong, and they just kept crashing against my barriers.

She had woken with confusion and it had quickly changed over to determination. I felt when the nervousness hit her and when a brief flare of anger filled her. I knew that she felt emotional pain, and then came the part that I didn't want to feel—the love, the happiness. I didn't want to be a part of that.

When the feelings of excitement rushed through our bond, I did everything I could to block it out. It was so painful, I wanted to curl up in a ball and hide.

She was with Julian now. She made her choice. I packed my clothes, hoping I would get it all done before she arrived here. It didn't matter that I had promised her I would wait. I couldn't see the look on her face. I couldn't stand to hear her say the words.

I grabbed my garment bag and black leather duffel bag and started down the stairs. As I did, I allowed the barrier to come down and felt her brief moment of nothing but happiness and longing.

I sighed and stepped out the front door. As I walked to my car, I heard a car start up the driveway. The deep sounds of the exhaust made its way up the hill. Was that her Challenger I heard?

She pulled up the driveway and I realized that she had made it home, found my note, and switched cars. I wasn't going to be able to get away from this. I steeled myself for what was coming.

She parked behind my car, blocking me from leaving. She sat in the driver's seat and looked at me through the windshield. Cautiously, she exited and approached me.

"You were going to leave." It wasn't a question. She stared at my bags.

I turned to open the trunk of my car. "Yeah, didn't think I needed to hear what you had to say. I'm pretty smart and I think I figured it out." I didn't look at her while I spoke; I just arranged my bags and closed the hatch.

"You have always underestimated me, you know that? You did back then, and you're doing it now," she said to my back.

I laughed and turned around; it wasn't a nice laugh. "And why would you think I used to underestimate you?"

"Because you spent so much time thinking I might not be strong enough to stand at your side, to help you with your job, to be there for you, to be your mate. But I was."

My eyes narrowed as I took in her determined stance, the look of heat in her eyes. *Wait a second*, I thought.

"Why are you talking in the past tense?" I asked her quietly.

She laughed and threw her hands up. "Because, Alexander, I remember everything. I remember every moment of my life as Kristin, and as Calista." She eyed me carefully.

"You do?" She remembered? If she remembered, then she knew that she had loved Julian; that she had chosen him instead.

"Yes, I do," she simply replied.

"Then what are you doing here? Why aren't you with Julian? I knew you went into his arms. I could feel the happiness you had being there." I was angry. I didn't want to go through this anymore. I just wanted it to stop.

"You need to stop eavesdropping on my emotions." She sighed as she glared at me. "I went to Julian, yes, but I went to tell him that it wasn't his fault that I had died. I was the one who found Damon and brought him to our house to see Julian."

She spoke confidently, strongly, and I was mesmerized by her. I didn't say anything; I didn't trust my voice. "I knew Julian was searching for him, and I thought it was because he was his son and not because he was trying to stop him from what he was doing. I went to Julian tonight to tell him to stop blaming himself. I had put myself in harm's way, it wasn't his fault."

"Why did you do that?" My hands were clenched at my sides.

"Because things weren't right with us, and I thought that maybe if I did something for him, things would be better. We both shared so much guilt about what had happened with you that it was coming between us."

I cleared my throat. "Fine. So now that you have had a chance to explain, you can go back to Julian." I turned away from her.

"Alex, stop!" I did—I did exactly what she told me. I stopped. I even held my breath. The pleading sound in her voice gave me an ounce of hope for a second.

"Look at me, Alex," she said quietly when I didn't turn around.

I did and she approached me. Her eyes were a beautiful, bright clear blue.

"Alex, I believe that I came back as a smarter, stronger person for two reasons. First, was to allow Julian to forgive himself, and second..." She stepped closer.

Her sweet scent flowed over me so fast that I thought I would fall to the ground. What was the emotion that was flowing over her?

"My second reason," she started again, "was to make right what had been so wrong in my life."

Was that emotion flowing over her...love? Could that possibly be for me? I swallowed, still not trusting myself to speak.

"Alex, I made such a horrible mistake. I know it, and Julian does, too. It was you that I should have been with. It was you that I should have mated with. It was you that I really wanted."

I was still holding my breath. She kept saying "was." What about now? I couldn't open my mouth to speak.

As if knowing what I needed to hear, she spoke softly. "It's you that I want. It's you that I have always ever really wanted. It is you that I love."

I looked at her, wanting to believe, but afraid that if I moved it would all vanish into a dream, and she would not really be there.

When I didn't speak, she spoke once more. "Alex, will you be my mate?"

Pure love and absolute nervousness washed over me from her. I reached forward for her, pulling her into my arms, crushing her to my body as my mouth found hers.

The kiss was deep, encompassing years of loss, years of wanting. I lifted her off the ground, easily picking her up in my arms and setting her on the back of my car.

Her arms were wrapped tightly around me, and as I seated her on the car, she wrapped her legs around my waist, pulling me closer with the strength of her leg muscles.

We pulled apart, both needing a moment to catch our breath, and she looked at me with a sparkle in her eye. "So, is that a yes?"

"I think I was supposed to be the one to ask that question." I smiled down at her. Even sitting up on the car, she was shorter than I was.

"Yeah—well, you should have asked me that about forty years ago. I figured since I came back a stronger and smarter woman, I'd do the asking this time." She winked at me.

I leaned down and kissed her one more time—gently, slowly, running my hands over her back. I moved my mouth away from her lips and to her ear and whispered, "Oh, yeah! That's a yes!"

I felt her whole body relax against mine, and as I continued to kiss her neck, I moved my mouth to the vein I felt pumping in her throat. I wanted to take her right this second. I didn't want to waste one more moment of my life without her.

As I closed in on her vein and opened my mouth, my fangs extending quickly—wanting to feed from her, needing to feed from her—she pushed me back.

At first, I didn't feel it, I was so focused on taking her vein, but when I realized what she was doing, I had a moment of panic. Maybe this really had all been a dream. I looked into her eyes and found them smiling back at me.

"Um...Alex. Would you mind if we did this someplace else?" she asked, laughing quietly as she said it.

I was confused, until she reached over and knocked on the trunk of the car.

"Um…It's kind of like 'been there done that,' and I'd like this to start off right, the way it should have been forty years ago." She gave me a seductive smile and it finally dawned on me what she was saying.

"Ever mated in a king-sized bed?" I asked her as I scooped her up in my arms and started carrying her to the house.

"Nope, sounds like the perfect place." She laid her head against my shoulder and sighed contentedly.

"No, the perfect place would be in our home in New York." I didn't realize the effect my words would have on her, and she stiffened in my arms.

I looked down at her as she said, "We aren't going to move there, are we?"

That was a strange question; why wouldn't we go to my home in New York? "Of course, I have to run the business," I said, smiling gently at her.

"But, Alex, my job is here." She was looking at me and I had stopped at the landing on the stairs to look down into her face.

"Kristin, if you want to work, you can work with me," I said gently to her.

"Alex, I'm a cop. I love my job. I might be about to turn into a full-blooded vampire, but I'm still a cop, and my blood runs blue."

I smiled down at her. "Kristin, if that is what you want to do, then we will figure it all out. Right now, all I want to do is sink my teeth into your neck and see what color your blood really is."

And with that, I strode off down the hall toward my chamber door, listening to her laugh gently in my arms as she rested her head against my chest.

The emotions of longing, love, and forever swirled around us, mixing in with the scents of butter, sugar, coffee, and spices.

CHAPTER THIRTY-TWO

KRISTIN

*I*t had been four weeks since the return of my memories. It hadn't been hard for Alex to get a doctor friend to write a letter telling my chief that I had been injured in an accident and I needed some time to recover from the concussion I had sustained.

It was enough time for me to begin my transition and for Alex and me to spend some much-needed time getting to know each other again.

I had not spoken to Julian since that night, and I knew that we both needed time to deal with what had happened. Alex said that Julian was taking a leave of absence, but that he would eventually be back. I knew that one day we would see each other again and it would be interesting to see what happened when we did.

Eventually, Alex and I decided that it would be good for me to get back to work. Alex wanted me to be happy and he knew that being back here at work would do that. I think he also wanted to get me back to work since I was bouncing off the walls without having anything to do. I know he was used to his privacy after so many years, and it would take us a while to get used to having another person in our lives.

We knew that we would see each other often, and we were only a single thought away from each other at any one time. That was something that had not been expected. When we mated, we had no idea that Alex's ability to read emotions as strongly as he could, would cross the bond so completely and bloom in me. Now, we merely had to think of loving each other and the feeling spread to the other person, no matter what the distance.

I could feel such a feeling now as I entered the door to my station. He was wishing me luck on my first shift back. I grinned to myself and sent him love back.

I had been lucky to get my chief to put me on a semi-permanent night shift. I told him that the sunlight still caused me headaches. The days would soon be getting shorter with fall coming soon, and the nights would allow me to work safely as my body continued to transition.

I wasn't sure what I would do come spring when the daylight started to exceed the dark, but I would cross that bridge when I came to it. For now, this worked fine, and I was happy to be back.

With a sense of pride and honor, I reached into my locker and pulled out my bulletproof vest. I pulled it over my head and laughed. I didn't really need it, but it would feel strange not to wear it after all these years. It would also raise questions, I was sure. I took my short-sleeved polo shirt off the hanger and pulled it on, allowing my hands to run down the front to smooth it out, stopping as it touched the silver embroidered badge over my left breast.

The badge was my pledge to serve and protect the citizens of my township and the commonwealth, and while I was no longer human, I still felt the need to protect those who needed my assistance. I would always feel the need to protect the innocent. I pulled on my duty belt, smiling as I adjusted it to my waist. God, it felt good to put it back on!

After looking through my mailbox and listening to a couple of messages, I knew it was time to make the one phone call that I had been putting off.

I picked up the phone and dialed a number I knew by heart, and after two rings, a man's voice answered the line.

"Detective Davis," he said.

"Jim, hey, it's Kristin Greene." I was smiling as I spoke. It was good to hear his voice.

"Kristin! How are you feeling? I heard about your accident."

"I'm great, Jim, better than ever, really." If he only knew just how true that really was. I laughed softly.

"Good! Glad to hear you are back. Hey, I'm glad you called, I wanted you to know what's been going on with the case." He hesitated, and I allowed him his time before he continued. "It's pretty amazing, but somehow there is absolutely no evidence or leads in any of the homicides that have occurred, and they seem to have stopped for now. Since we don't have anything to go on, we basically are going to have to put them on the back burner until something else happens." Like any good investigator, he seemed frustrated by this.

"Wow, nothing, huh?" I knew there wasn't anything they would have found, or anything that they would ever find. There wouldn't be any more homicides like this in the future, not with Damon dead for good.

"Funny thing is that none of the families seemed to be upset when we told them we have nothing to go on. It's like they have all already moved on and aren't worried about it." He sighed into the phone.

He had no clue that the families had already received their justice when Julian had ended Damon's existence. They already had the closure that they wanted and needed.

I spoke with Jim for a few more minutes before hanging up. Since I was back, I didn't feel like sitting around the station; I wanted to get out on the street and put my new senses to work.

I walked out the door of the station, climbed into the Expedition, and looked out the windshield. As I turned on the truck, I knew that for the first time I would patrol my township not wondering what was missing from my life but thinking about all that I had in it.

I put the truck in gear, and my radio called out over the speaker behind me, "Thirty-One-Paul-One."

I smiled and reached for my mic. It was damn good to be back.

THE END

My Blood Runs Blue, Book 1

Officer Kristin Greene has always felt that something was missing from her life. Although her job with the Fawn Hollow Township Police Department keeps her busy, she still feels like there is something else out there for her.

She soon finds herself investigating a homicide where a young woman has had her throat ripped out. As she begins to dig for the answers, she finds herself thrown into a world she didn't know ever existed.

When the two strong and silent men walk into her life, she finds herself being pulled into a love triangle that has been going on longer than she has been alive. Who are they and why do they keep calling her Calista?

Join Kristin as she fights to learn the truth about the recent murder, the two seductive men who have entered into her life and the real truth about herself.

The Pulse of Blue Blood, Book 2

The Pulse of Blue Blood is a short story that should be read AFTER My Blood Runs Blue. This story of 17K words is the back story to Kristin & Calista. Reading this story before reading My Blood Runs Blue will spoil many plot points.

In My Blood Runs Blue, you were introduced to Kristin, Julian, and Alexander, and you also learned a little about Calista.

Now take a trip back in time to learn more about the decisions that Calista made in her choice between Julian and Alexander.

Learn about her relationship with Julian, and why you choose Alexander at the end of My Blood Runs Blue. You'll also learn the way she caused her untimely death.

The Pulse of Blue Blood is a short story to be read after reading My Blood Runs Blue.

Blue Blood for Life, Book 3

After a month off, Kristin comes back to work happier then she's been in a long time. Her new status in life has her solving crimes faster and better than she ever could before.

When Alex goes missing, Kristin finds she finally has to reveal the secrets of her life to her friends. Will they be able to stand beside her after they learn all that she has hidden from them?

Julian and Gabe stand beside her faithfully as they try to locate Alex. They are surprised to find Trent already in Fawn Hollow, but know that Trent may be the only one to do what Alex has asked them to do. As one more choice is taken away from Kristin, she attempts to make the best of it, but finds herself drawn to Trent in a way Julian and Alexander could never compare to.

Trent goes to work with Kristin to keep her safe but will he be able to handle all that her police world entails? Can he handle the side of her that she reveals, the one that Alex and Julian know nothing about? When Kristin and Trent uncover the connection between her job and the kidnapping, they are finally able to put the pieces together, but can they get to Alex fast enough? Will Kristin be able to handle rescuing Alex and all that she learns in the process?

Join Kristin, Julian, Trent and Alexander as they dive into a new mystery that will have you turning the pages quickly to find out who is responsible and how Kristin's life is forever changed once again.

Mixing the Blue Blood, Book 4

Officer Kristin Greene returns along with the rest of the characters you have grown to love. Only this time, it's not just her life on the line. Now the entire breed's existence is in danger.

Olivia Newman has been Kristin's best friend for years and loves the new life that Kristin is living. Her relationship with Gabriel is bittersweet, and she knows that because she is human, a future between them can never really last.

Gabriel Montgomery takes his position in the Vampire Military Force seriously and never expected to have such intense feelings for a human woman. When Olivia is kidnapped, Gabe, Kristin, and the gang realize they have stumbled upon a human trafficking ring. Only this ring isn't for sex. The leaders of this ring are hell-bent on destroying the breed.

Can they rescue Olivia and save their future before old enemies return and destroy the breed? Find out in Mixing the Blue Blood.

Blue Bloods Final Destiny, Book 5

Julian Hutchinson walked away from it all: his job, his friends and her. As Julian drives out west, he randomly stops at a roadside tavern and runs into some people from his past.

Ellie Lakin helps her father around the tavern as she raises her fifteen-year-old daughter, Lorna. When Julian walks into the bar, Ellie's past crush on him hits full force, but even she can tell that he is far from ready to be involved with anyone.

As Julian and Ellie grow their friendship their past romance is rekindled. When Julian's past comes back to haunt him, and an old enemy shows up in town, Julian knows a showdown is imminent. Will

Julian be able to deal with his past, and his enemy without destroying the new life he has created.

The gang is back for one final book where lines are drawn and quickly crossed, and Julian and Kristin will have to work together one last time to save people that they care about.

The Return of Blue Blood Series:
Kristin: Blue Blood Returns, Book 1
Hugh: Blue Blood Compelled, Book 2
Zander: Blue Blood Reborn, Book 3
Lena: Blue Blood Desired, Book 4 (coming soon)

BOOKS BY STACY EATON

Download a FREE Series Guide of books written by Stacy Eaton
ROMANCE TO GET YOUR BLOOD PUMPING
This guide includes a listing of all of her current books and upcoming releases. It includes genre's, heat levels, series links to other series, and the first chapter of almost all of the books.

Rise Again Warrior Series
Mission: Believe, Book 1 **
Mission: Accept, Book 2 **
Mission: Repair, Book 3

Loving a Young Series
Wesley, Book 1
Henley, Book 2
Huntley, Book 3
Riley, Book 4
Kayley, Book 5
Bradley, Book 6 (coming soon)

The Unexpected Series
Unexpected Packages
Unexpected Arrivals
Unexpected Trouble
Unexpected Storms
Unexpected Desires
Unexpected Ties (coming soon)

Paranormal Romance:
My Blood Runs Blue Series
My Blood Runs Blue, Book 1 **
The Pulse of Blue Blood, Book 2 (Short Story) **
Blue Blood for Life, Book 3 **
Mixing the Blue Blood, Book 4 **
Blue Bloods Final Destiny, Book 5 **

The Return of Blue Blood Series:
Kristin: Blue Blood Returns, Book 1
Hugh: Blue Blood Compelled, Book 2
Zander: Blue Blood Reborn, Book 3
Lena: Blue Blood Desired, Book 4 (coming soon)

Garda ~ Welcome to the Realm

The Twisted Love Series
with Amy Manemann Co-Author
Love Lorn, Book 1 (Manemann)**
Love Torn, Book 2 (Eaton)**
Love Inked, Book 3
Love Drowned, Book 4
Love Carved, Book 5
Love Trapped, Book 6
Love Crossed, Book 7 (Coming Soon)
Love Twisted, Book 8 (Coming Soon)
Love Lies, Book 9 (Coming Soon)

Domestic Violence – Crime - Suspense:
Whether I'll Live or Die**
Barbara's Plea
You're Not Alone**

Romantic Suspense:
Liveon ~ No Evil **
Second Shield ***
Distorted Loyalty**
Six Days of Memories **
Second Shield II: The Return ***

Contemporary Romance:
Tempt Me Too**
Finding the Strength

Finding Love in Special Places:
Stacy's Short Story Series
Finding Love on Christmas Vacation
Finding Love on the Summer Surf
Finding Love with Dear Santa
Finding Love with a Champagne Toast

Heart of the Family Series
Mistletoe & Cocoa Kisses, Book 1 **
Roses & Champagne Kisses, Book 2 **
Orchids & Hurricane Kisses, Book 3 **
Carnations & Hot Toddy Kisses, Book 4 **

Heal Me Series
Cured, Book 1 **
Revived, Book 2
Mended, Book 3
Rescued, Book 4

The Celebration Series
Tangled in Tinsel, Book 1 **
Tears to Cheers, Book 2 **
Heathens to Hearts, Book 3 **
Rainbows Bring Riches, Book 4 ***
Sweet as Sugar, Book 5 ***
Making Mom Mad, Book 6 ***
Sparklers or Spankings, Book 7 ***
Raffles to Rattles, Book 8 ***
Flirting with Fireworks, Book 9 ***
Working under Wheels, Book 10 ***
Masquerading at Midnight, Book 11 ***
Blessings & Beans, Book 12 ***
Velvet & Vows, Book 13 ***

The Celebration Series Box Sets:
Part One: Books 1-5
Part Two: Books 6-9
Part Three: Books 10-13

The Sometimes Series:
Sometimes You Win, Book 1**
Sometimes You Lose, Book 2**
Sometimes You Play The Game, Book 3**
The Sometimes Series: Win, Lose & Play Set **

Pleasure Your Fantasies Series
Mistletoe Fantasies, Book 1 **
Whispered Fantasies, Book 2
Secret Fantasies, Book 3

** These books are also available on Audio
*** These books are coming to Audio soon
List Update 3-10-21

ABOUT THE AUTHOR

Stacy Eaton is a USA Today Best Selling author and began her writing career in October of 2010. Stacy took an early retirement from law enforcement after over fifteen years of service in 2016, with her last three years in investigations and crime scene investigation to write full time.

Stacy resides in southeastern Pennsylvania with her husband, who works in law enforcement, and her teen daughter. She also has a son who is currently serving in the United States Navy and has two grandchildren.

Be sure to visit www.stacyeaton.com for updates and more information on her books.

Sign up for all the latest information on Stacy's Newsletter!

facebook.com/stacyeatonauthor

twitter.com/StacySEaton

instagram.com/authorstacyeaton

www.ingramcontent.com/pod-product-compliance
Lightning Source LLC
Chambersburg PA
CBHW050042180626
46810CB00002B/850